ADAM EXITUS

Book One:

Adam X Series

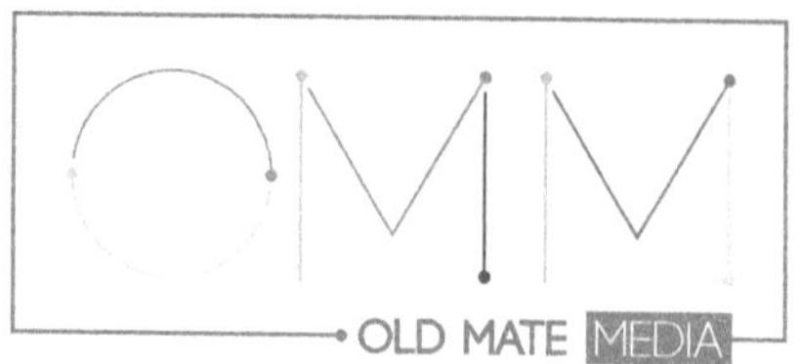

Written, Conceived and Illustrated by
NICHOLAS ABDILLA

Edited and Designed by
CHRIS STEAD

Published by
OLD MATE MEDIA
www.oldmatemedia.com

ISBN: 978-1-925638-00-4

DEDICATED TO SIA, ANGELINA AND HARRISON

FOREWORD

I can still remember the exact day I created Adam X.
It was June 6, 2006.

I had just spent three years on a graphic novel called
OCD, which was all about the struggles of living
with depression and anxiety. After spending so long
working with such heavy subject matter, I really
needed a change. I began to feel like it was time to
create something a little more light-hearted and fun.

As a writer I was determined to create a new comic
book series that combined all of my interests into one
neat package. Something that didn't force me to stick
to just one genre. As an artist I wanted a relevant
reason to draw all the crazy stuff that popped into my
head on a daily basis.

With those two goals firmly in mind the Adam X
universe was born.

Ten years and ten books later, the Adam-verse has
grown into a place of infinite possibilities. Adam's
world has given me the opportunity to write mysteries,
romances, tragedies and, of course, science-fiction.
While drawing the book has allowed my imagination to
run wild as it consistently provides the opportunity to
create interesting new creatures to populate the world.

But in the end it was Adam himself that made this series such an intense joy to write. Unlike all the super-powered and supernatural characters I've created over the past two decades, Adam remains at his core a regular guy. Just an ordinary man dealing with an extraordinary situation.

He is relatable, and I think that's why he resonates with me as strongly today as he did back in 2006.

I'd like to welcome those reading the series for the first time and thank those of you who have been following Adam's story over the years. I hope you enjoy this novelisation of his first adventure and I look forward to diving into the Adam-verse again with you soon.

PROLOGUE

It always starts and ends the same way. Beginning with terror; ending with blood.

Where am I?

Someone is watching. Always watching. In the shadows; in the lights. Those bright lights. Swirling with the cold spiralling up my spine.

Who are you?

I stand on the edge of a precipice, wind tugging at my hair. I leap off. My head splits open like a melon, my brains splattered on the rocks below. The world stands sideways, unmoved as I blink it all away.

Am I dead?

No. It isn't over. I try again. Diving off the same cliff. This time I break my spine. I hear the crack echo over and over again. My internal organs haemorrhage. Air explodes from my lungs out into the lights.

Why am I still here?

A woman's voice speaks harsh truths. I don't wish to hear them. I silently scream into the dark and the sound is defeaning. I tie a vine around my neck and use it to asphyxiate myself.

Will her words ever cease?

I mistake silence for peace. I fool myself for a time, refusing to see reality for what it is. My skin wrinkles and my hair goes grey. My heart seizes and I exhale my last breath. There, I did it. This is finally the end.

No.

Even age will not end my torment. I'm still here. I'm still screaming. Beasts now tear at my flesh and infection sets in my wounds. Death is inevitable: I can feel the black slithering through my veins and I invite it deeper. This is it.

Then from the lights an unlikely saviour; but it's a rescue unwelcomed.

What do you want from me?

But this is no angel. Saviour just means delay, and my suffering continues. Poisoned and mauled.

It's torture.

Will it always start and end the same way? Terror, blood. Terror, blood. Can anything break this endless cycle? Am I destined to do this forever? It didn't used to be like this, I'm sure. Now I'm drowning. Is that blood in my lungs?

Is this it?

No, the lights. Not again. I scream, for real this time. Will they always just watch? Who are you? I look for help and spot her. The woman: she's right there. I reach out and she takes my hand.

What's happening?

But the woman stands silent and I feel it start again.

Terror.

I

Sitting with my back against the cold hard stone, I twirl a small piece of chalk between my thumb and forefinger absentmindedly.

Why is this happening?

My mind ponders our predicament for the millionth time, and just like every other time I ask this question only silence responds. Nothing about this situation makes any sense.

Fourteen days ago I fell asleep in my small, one bedroom apartment amongst a jumble of pillows and blankets. Same as always. But I awoke not to the incessant sounds of my alarm clock drilling into my ears. Instead I found myself lying face down in the middle of a jungle, stripped of all my possessions, and just plain stripped.

Left for dead.

Why choose to do this to me? It's not like I'm somebody important.

I have only just graduated from the academy after all. So I haven't yet had the time required to make genuine enemies in the criminal underworld.

Besides, who kidnaps a police officer? What motive could there possibly be?

I have no wealth to speak of, so it's not like this could be about money.

Also, how do you move someone all the way out here without waking them up? And where the hell is "here" anyway?

Judging by my surroundings, I can't even be sure I'm in the same country anymore. But of all the questions swirling around inside my brain like draining bathwater, the strangest one of all would have to do with the X. Why did they tattoo an X on my forehead?

If it's some great treasure they're hoping to find in there, well I'm afraid my captors are gonna be sadly disappointed!

I chuckle at the thought, and the pathetic sound bounces off the cave walls, echoing into the abyss.

It was on the second day that I first noticed my new ink. My throat, dryer than sandpaper and just as coarse, yearned for liquid, so I finally gave in and drank from the lagoon. And there it was staring back at me in my reflection.

My abductors had marked me, and no amount of scrubbing since had been able to erase the cross on my brow. On the positive side, at least I was able to keep down that dodgy looking water.

What does it all mean?

Climbing onto the balls of my feet I turn around and crouch in front of the wall that had so admirably supported my weight for the better part of the past two weeks. The chalk feels soft in my fingers, now powdered from all the twiddling. With what little of it remains, I scratch a message onto the stone:

Adam Furst Was Here

Not the most original sentiment I'll admit, but it's the best I can come up with. I imagine an explorer coming along many years from now and discovering my skeletal remains laying in front of it – my lame last words to the world.

My morbid thoughts are interrupted by the arrival of my only other companion. She strolls gracefully into our dank cave, past the roaring waterfall that hides the entrance. Her hair glistens from the newly nestled spray, hogging what little light splinters through the sheet of water. A dead boar is draped over her shoulders, like some grotesque fashion accessory.

Great!

"Wild pig for dinner again I see," fumble the words from my mouth. A greeting that's little more than a feeble attempt to shake off my dark mood.

She probably couldn't even hear it over that incessant waterfall.

"You'll have to show me how you catch those sometime," I try a little louder, and with more enthusiasm. But silent as always, she drops the carcass to the floor and barely gives my request the courtesy of a glance. And what glance she did offer said all I needed to hear on the subject.

I guess I haven't done much to show her I am capable of such action.

She picks up a sharp stone – the same one from yesterday – and starts using it to gut the poor beast. The first drops of blood begin pooling in the dimples of the cave's floor.

Why couldn't she do that outside? Seriously?

She rolls the poor creature over and I see the scars. A series of them across its belly. I cock my head sideways for a better look. They almost look like letters.

M, I and X. Mix? Mix with what? Mix with basil? Or with potatoes. They can't really be letters, can they?

She slices straight down its stomach before I can be sure and my absent musings turn to disgust as blood and entrails start to press through the open wound. Bile begins to bubble at the base of my throat.

I need a distraction quick or I'm gonna puke.

I turn my attention away from the gruesome scene and focus instead on her. I notice not for the first time how truly beautiful she is. Sparkling sapphire eyes, pouty lips and straight chestnut brown hair that hangs down to the small of her back. I found her cooking over a fire my first night here and she has kept me fed and warm ever since.

She belongs on a runway, not stuck in this godforsaken place with me.

Her alabaster skin is flawless apart from a faint circular scar on her forehead. It's in the exact same place as my X, I suddenly realise.

Whoever put us here has a disturbingly sick sense of humour.

Why brand us both like this? Branding her, at least, anyway – why spoil perfection?

Her fur coverings leave very little to the imagination and as my eyes drift down to her ample bosom I become uncomfortably aware that I too am only wearing a loincloth. She made it for me on that first day. I look away from her and place my focus back on the butchery as I wait for the feeling to subside.

As soon as she is done disembowelling the beast she leaves again. Off to find firewood so she can cook our meal, I suspect. I follow, desperate for the companionship and conversation. Even if that conversation is one-sided.

"Hey! Look what I found: chalk," I call after her as we exit through the spray curtain. I'm sure my words are drowned out by the thundering death rolls of the collapsing river, until she pauses and turns.

"I know you're not big on the whole talking thing," I continue, "but I thought you could use it to write your name for me. You know mine, but I still don't know what to call you."

Regarding me coolly for a moment, she washes the blood from her hands in one of the pools left by the waterfall and then takes the chalk. Heading over to a nearby tree, she brushes off a layer of bark and manages to scratch out the letter A and N before the tiny stub crumbles into nothingness.

> *Damn! I shouldn't have wasted it writing that stupid message on the wall.*

"Oh well, it's a start. Shouldn't be too hard to work out now that I have something to go off. Um... let's see. Is it... Angelina?"

She shakes her head, no.

"Andrea?"

Another no.

"Annabelle?"

No again.

"Anastasia?"

Nope.

"How about I just call you Anne for now? Is that ok?"

She nods yes and I grin for the first time in a while. In fact, I can feel the muscles around my jaw strain with the unfamiliar gesture, but I welcome the pain. I'm happy to have a name to go with that beautiful face.

I need to keep this conversation rolling. I need to prove I have some worth.

"Look, I owe you for keeping me alive this long. I wouldn't have lasted out here without you, not in the state you found me. But I'm feeling better now, stronger, and we can't just sit around waiting to get rescued. Starting tomorrow we're leaving this lagoon and finding a way out of this jungle. I will get you out of here, Anne. I swear it."

Or die trying.

She stares blankly at me for a moment as if to call my bluff. Then I realise her look is little more than an exaggeration of the glance delivered moments earlier in the cave.

Did that sound too macho?

But all too quickly she turns away and resumes searching the dry brush for firewood, seemingly unmoved by my impassioned speech. Silence descends on us again. Her despondence makes me wonder how long she's been trapped in this horrible place. The thought sends a shiver down my spine, but steels my resolve.

I will get you home. You and I both.

XXXX

I'm awake before the sun rises: mind racing like a cockroach scurrying for cover. As soon as the first rays of sunshine creep through our watery front door I'm up, determined to make good on my promise. I stuff a quick breakfast of nuts and berries into my face and answer nature's call behind a tree.

Now to launch straight into my escape plan. After a night of restless thought, I'd decided our first step to freedom was to map out our surroundings and get our bearings. Starting from the cave, with the waterfall and its cliff at my back, I head east in a straight line.

The dense foliage and vines ensure progress is slow. Thorns reach out and leave claw marks in my exposed flesh while sharp rocks dig into my feet. Soon they are bloody and raw, my skin a criss-crossed pattern of pain. In fact, I'm a mess: not one part of my exposed flesh has retained its pinkish-white hue.

Thank God for this loincloth!

I press on stubbornly refusing to let nature break my resolve. Anne handles the trek with far more poise, of course. The jungle almost parts for her as she follows in the wake of my flailing and cursing without so much as a whimper. She navigates the jungle with practiced ease, occasionally grabbing my shoulder and pointing out a threat I'd totally failed to notice and steering me around it.

What the hell am I doing out here?

I'm grateful for her help, especially when her quick tug at my arm prevents me from stepping on a snake. The brightly coloured red and yellow bands running down the length of the reptile's body probably should have given it away.

As we watch the serpent slither off into the foliage I'm reminded of a rhyme my stepfather –Nigel Mann, a brigadier in the British Armed Forces – taught me on one of our many camping expeditions.

Red on black, venom lack;
red on yellow, deadly fellow.

I always hated it when my stepdad would drag my mother and I on one of those awful trips, but what I learned from him might just save my life out here. With that sobering thought locked firmly in mind, I proceed with renewed caution.

By midday we reach a clearing and a sheer drop that I'm not confident I could get down even if I had climbing gear. Over the edge I see more jungle stretching out as far as the eye can see; giant trees made to look small by the distance. I strain my eyes, but there's not a manmade structure to be seen. The vista reminds me of pictures of South America.

But I can't be that far away from home, it's simply not possible.

South America seems like a stretch. That would mean I was snatched from my home and, somehow, kept unconscious for an entire flight over the Pacific Ocean. All that before being unceremoniously dumped on an entirely new continent. Dumped on my face, no less. In the mud.

Unable to go up or down I decide to follow the top of the cliff, hoping to find somewhere safer to climb down. The face remains sheer, though. Stepping near the edge encourages a squadron of loose rocks to plummet to a dusty doom on the canopy far below.

The whole time Anne watches me like a hawk, her arm shooting out protectively, but unnecessarily, a few times as I make my way along the edge. What's her problem? As if I'm not even capable of walking along a cliff without toppling over.

Why is she so spooked all of a sudden?

I realise then that I am limping badly, and with that recognition comes a wave of pain. I look towards Anne and if her feet are damaged at all from the brutality of our journey, it's not showing.

I must keep going.

Eventually our path is blocked by a roaring river that plunges over the edge unfazed by the drop. Something stuck in a collection of twigs at the precipice catches my eye, wedged between two rocks… is that skin?

It's the remains of the boar, you fool. Last night's dinner. This river leads right back to the lagoon!

My heart sinks and for a second my frustration threatens to get the best of me. Anne says nothing, of course, but her glance at the setting sun tells me all I need to know about her position on the matter. Dejected and not wanting to be without shelter for the night, we spend the remainder of the day following the bank back up stream.

At least the sand feels good.

It's dark by the time we end up where we started and I immediately head inside our cave, our home, without saying a word. Sleep is hard to come by again, but excitement is no longer the cause. I'm sore, hungry and extremely discouraged.

If the first day of scouting was disheartening, then the second was downright depressing. Heading towards the west from our cave only served up more cuts and bruises, followed by another sheer drop. And yet again, following the cliff top only brought us to a river barrier, which wound its way back to the lagoon.

The same damn lagoon, endlessly refilled by our makeshift front door.

The inescapable conclusion to all this adventuring was clear – our entire jungle home is perched on a large rock ledge. And that ledge is stuck to the face of a massive cliff that rises unscaleable towards the clouds in one direction, and dangerously towards the valley in the other.

This is a prison.

I rub at the X on my forehead as my eyes flick towards Anne, silently watching my turmoil etch its story into my face. She would have known all along. She would have explored. She would have come to the same conclusion. But what choice did she have but to let me find out for myself?

That night, as I stared into the campfire absently scratching at the itchy beard now carpeting my face, the truth washed over me like a tidal wave. The facts were undeniable.

We're backed against a cliff with sheer drops on all sides, which means there's no way we're getting out of here on foot.

It can't be just a simple coincidence that I was placed here. It's the perfect location to keep a person trapped.

Or two people, as it turns out. Yet the sheer logistics of pulling something like this off are baffling. I mean, did they use a plane to fly me up here then drop me into the jungle by parachute?

No, if that were the case I would've been draped in the open chute when I awoke.

Maybe they flew me here by helicopter?

That can't be right. They would need some kind of clearing to land in and I haven't found anywhere that isn't densely packed with trees.

Maybe they just threw me out the door? That would somewhat explain the weird pain I felt when I gained consciousness. Also my weakened condition. Regardless, wouldn't it be easier to chain me to a radiator in some basement if imprisonment was the only goal?

It's not like I have a phone they can contact me on. How are they going to communicate their demands?

I look up from the flames and fix my gaze squarely on Anne. She is busy cooking a freshly plucked chicken over the fire, using a crude contraption made of sticks. But even that basic human activity feels beyond my skills. There was nothing in my training to prepare me for this.

What's her deal exactly?

I was so quick to trust her, but what do I really know about this woman? For all I know she's in cahoots with my abductors. They must have someone on the ground. This mute caretaker routine is probably an act meant to keep me docile until they decide what to do.

Every day she disappears into the jungle with no tools, yet somehow returns with food.

Perhaps she's secretly meeting the masterminds behind my abduction and they're providing us with our meals. The more I think about it the more it makes sense. How could one woman survive out here alone for so long? And still be so cool, calm and collected – there's barely a mark on her.

She's behind this.

I'm startled from my reverie when she stands suddenly. Walking over from her spot across from the fire she offers me a leg that smells so good it makes my mouth water. It's cooked to perfection.

"Thanks, but I've lost my appetite," I lie, forcing a smile.

I refuse to take anything more from this woman until I know she's on the level.

So I sit there stubbornly while my stomach growls in protest, but Anne just shrugs and devours her chicken as I watch on. Absent-minded, I rub at the X on my head. Hard.

Tomorrow I'll expose you.

‖

I drop down into my pile of straw and animal skins at the back of our cave, eyes closed, but ears open. I listen to Anne, who lays on her own bedding, just metres away.

Shouldn't be too much longer now.

She remains eerily still and silent for many hours. Staring through the dark at her, I pass the time by coming up with conspiracy theories.

My fingers fiddle with my bedding as I begin wondering if anyone back home has noticed my absence. My mother – a former military nurse named Henrietta Furst – moved back to Munich a few years ago after she separated with my stepfather.

Since then we would be lucky to speak once a month, so it's unlikely she's noticed I've gone missing.

I should've called her more often.

Perhaps my captain? Hopefully. I recall my surly boss sitting there – stiff of neck and quick to yell – embedded behind that old, giant desk back at the station. Surely he must've noticed I didn't return to work on the date we agreed.

Or not.

It isn't a certainty. We didn't exactly part on the best of terms. In fact, he is just as likely to interpret my absence as an unofficial resignation. There would be no cause for concern; he probably even feels like I've made another tough conversation easier.

Forced leave is about as good as being fired anyway, right?

It's just before daybreak when I'm snapped out of my deliberation by the rustle of warm animal furs against cold stone. Anne has finally stirred. I remain still, feigning sleep during a moment of painful silence. The scratches on my feet and arms suddenly begin to itch like crazy.

Wait, am I breathing like a sleeping person?

I dare a quick peek from beneath a lazy eyelid and watch as she exits through the waterfall.

Get up you idiot, quick!

Brushing away a stray piece of straw camped and camouflaged against my sandy, blonde hair, I creep along the cave wall and peer cautiously outside. It's still dark out, but I can just about make out Anne's silhouette heading down the river.

Most likely in search of breakfast, like she does every morning.

It occurs to me all of a sudden that she might be off to relieve herself. I blush at the thought of having to watch during her private moments and a wave of doubt washes over me.

Maybe I'm just being paranoid? But there's only one way to sure.

Thankfully she doesn't seem to need a bathroom break. I watch her hunt from a discreet distance and begin to feel the fool. There's no delivery service bringing us our next feed, that's for sure. Although with no spear or weapon, I'm still not sure how she intends to catch breakfast.

Is she that good she can use her hands?

As the sun completes its indolent rise over the horizon it banishes the predawn gloom, forcing me to use the thickest of trees to stay hidden.

I was wrong. She's been nothing but good to me and this is how I repay her.

I realise how hungry I am and my thoughts drift to the night before, staring daggers at Anne while she gnawed on that juicy chicken. I'm just starting to harvest thoughts of slipping back to the cave when Anne freezes and begins glancing around anxiously.

Did my grumbling stomach give me away?

Ducking deeper behind a large fern I try to stay still. But soon her gaze settles in my general direction.

Can she see me? Surely not.

I freeze, but slowly Anne's arm comes up. She points at me and that's when all hell breaks loose – the next second stretches out into an eternity

I spot movement in my peripheral vision. The bush next to me shakes and I cock an eye in its direction, but dread is already wrestling my soul.

A huge mouth full of razor-sharp teeth leaps through the brush ready to strike. Adrenaline floods my body. I yelp and raise my hands in a futile attempt to protect myself from the attack. Thunder cracks. A beam of light strikes the predator mid leap. Its jaws snap shut just shy of my face and its large body slams into my side. The air in my lungs bursts from my body in a mad rush for freedom.

What the...?

We both hit the ground hard, a tangle of flailing limbs, dark scales and scattered thoughts.

XXXX

Winded, I push the heavy beast off me and scramble frantically away, my heart hammering in my chest. It makes no move to pursue and I realise with great relief that it's dead. Rational thought starts grasping at my brain, but can't get a grip.

Is this really happening?!

I try desperately to process the completely irrational scene before me. There is all of six-feet of velociraptor laying in the dirt only inches away from my feet. It looks like a discarded prop from some blockbuster Hollywood movie, but it's real. I can smell the stench of its breath on my face… it tried to eat me.

I was almost eaten!

Slowly my gaze settles on the wound. Smoke is rising from a small circular gash in the raptor's side where that freak energy discharge, or whatever it was, struck. The air simmers with the aroma of burnt ozone and cooked flesh.

As I gape at the dead dinosaur, Anne rushes to my side and offers to help me up. I reach for her outstretched hand, but then pull back in horror. Her open palm is smoking, just like the wound in the raptor's rib cage.

"You stay away from me," I gasp, pointing an accusing finger and helping myself up.

My legs feel like jelly.

Slowly I get my balance. My hearing is off. I backpedal haphazardly, but Anne's sure-footed steps are closing the distance quickly. Black dots begin to swarm my vision. But as soon as I am steady on my feet, I do the only thing that makes sense. I run.

XXXX

Low hanging vines and branches slap my face and shoulders as I make a mad dash through the jungle trying to flee the craziness behind me.

Run, Adam! Run!

I hear her footfalls behind me, she's close. But adrenalin is willing my body to a speed I never thought possible. Suddenly I burst free from the thick wall of plant life and in my blind rush almost run straight off the cliff that acts as my prison's wall. I skid to a halt, sliding along on the granules right to the very edge, only to watch as the small stones plummet down into the depths below.

Stepping back from the precipice I wipe perspiration from my eyes with shaky hands and try to slow my racing heart. Two near death experiences in as many minutes are too much, however. I vomit bile up out of my empty stomach, all over the grass.

A large shadow passes overhead and I squint up into the sun to see what is either a really large bird or – more disturbingly – a regular sized pterodactyl. A thought that would have been insane to me only moments earlier.

You're asleep! You have to be!

I desperately try to convince myself that I'm dreaming. Maybe I was shot in the line of duty and right now I'm lying in a hospital bed trapped in a coma.

What could be the alternative? I've travelled back in time?

The more I think about it the more sure I become. This isn't real. It's just some deranged coma nightmare. Nothing but a dream. That would explain the super-hot femme fatale, too. I laugh out loud at the realisation. I laugh hard.

If you jump off this cliff you'll wake up.

I creep an inch closer to the cliff's edge. My mind is a mess. I look down and can already feel it rushing towards me and realise that I have no fear. It will be ok, I'll wake up. I inch even closer.

And if you don't wake up, at least this will finally be over...

"Please step away from the cliff," a woman's voice pleads. I turn to see Anne approaching cautiously through the exit door of snapped branches I had left on my wild escape.

"You spoke!" I blurt out. "It doesn't matter. You're not real. None of this is real."

"I can confirm that I am very real. That is a real cliff. And there is a very logical explanation for all of this."

Oh that's reassuring.

I edge closer again and she halts her advance. "You mean, a logical explanation for how you shot a dinosaur with magic lightning from your finger? This ought to be good."

"My laser cannon fires from my palm not my finger," she offers in defiance of my sarcasm. "I was left with no alternative. It was the only way to protect you from that carnivorous reptile."

"You mean the velociraptor?" I ask incredulously. "The reptile wiped from Earth sixty million years ago!"

"Seventy-one million years to be more precise," Anne returns without pause.

"Oh well I'll remember that for my next trivia night," I squeeze out between pants. They didn't train us for this. Anne just stares at me; an emotional black hole. My eyes lock onto her hand.

"Laser cannon," I repeat, eyebrows arched in surprise. "So what does that make you?"

"I am an android," she replies, deadpan. "My primary function is to ensure your survival."

"Right, sure you are. And I'm the Easter Bunny!" spit the words through the sardonic smile crossing my lips. "Let's say for just one second I believe that you really are a robot…"

"Android," she corrects.

"Ok, whatever. Why are you telling me now? Why not last week? Or the week before? Or how about the instant I came stumbling into that cave seconds from death and begging for food? Straight after the bit where I said, 'Hi, I'm Adam.'"

"My secondary function was to maintain the illusion that we are in your natural habitat as long as doing so did not endanger your life. When it appeared that you would self-terminate just now, I felt it was necessary to abort that mission in favour of my primary objective."

"What do you mean illusion?" I dart my eyes quickly around the landscape to make sure it is still there. "Where are we?"

"We are currently aboard a spacecraft approximately ten-thousand light years from the planet you know as Earth," Anne responds.

This is nuts!

I stare blankly for a moment into her impossibly blue eyes. A and N she had started when writing her name, and I went with Anne – was she actually trying to write android? I burst into fits of laughter and tears rally to my eyes. Her story is just so ridiculous it takes me a full minute to regain enough composure to continue our conversation.

It can't possibly be true. Can it?

"You... You expect me to believe I've been abducted by aliens and that we're on a UFO?" I ask, breathlessly trying to hold back the giggles.

"No," she counters. "The abbreviation UFO implies that the object is unidentified and I am very much aware of this ship's identity."

"Ah-huh. Ok, *Anne-droid.* Prove it." I hold out my arms to exaggerate my request. "Why don't you show me the rest of your ship?"

"No. You are not allowed to leave this enclosure," comes the predictable response.

"That's convenient. Ok, let me put it another way. If you don't show me, I'm going to swan dive off this cliff. Does that compute?" I turn to face the edge again, swinging my arms in preparation.

"I'm going to do it," I tell her, hoping my mock diving gestures emphasise the point. "If you're really programmed to keep me alive you would have no choice but to do what I say. Am I right?"

She seems to ponder this for a moment. "You are correct. I will comply."

I watch in disbelief as the circular mark on Anne's head starts to glow and emit an ominous hum. Soon the light grows so bright I'm forced to look away as its heat toasts the hairs on my arms. The humming becomes so intense I can feel it vibrating my teeth.

What now?!

Then, just when I think my skull might crack from the pressure, the sensory onslaught fades. When I look back a doorway made of pure light has materialised in the space between Anne and I.

I rub at the mark on my forehead as I try and pierce the light and see through the door with my lame human eyes.

"This can't possibly be true." The words fall from my mouth in shock.

"Of course it is. I am incapable of lying," she informs me, as she makes her way around the entrance to stand by my side.

"That may be, but you aren't exactly forthcoming with the truth," I point out to no response. I take a second to consider all that has happened in the two weeks since I first met Anne. Her emotionless reaction to my passionate hero's speech suddenly makes sense. Her nights lying motionless and deathly silent by my side. Catching animals without a spear. That, beautiful unmarked skin: no wonder she never so much as limped since I met her.

And here I was worried I'd catch her going to the toilet.

Anne studies my face as the dots begin to join in my mind. "Are you ready to see the rest of the ship now?" she asks. Staring with childlike wonder and mouth agape, I slowly nod that I am.

After I take a few laps around the portal to confirm that it's not actually connected to anything, I finally build up enough courage to step through.

As I make my approach I feel all the tiny hairs on my arms and legs standing on end, tingling like an army of nervous soldiers. My body is bathed in a warmth that is not altogether unpleasant, and for a second it lulls me into believing it's actually going to be alright.

But the moment my head touches the light an uncomfortable pressure begins to build up in my skull. It reminds me of the feeling of descending from altitude in a small aeroplane. I begin shifting my jaw up and down in an attempt to make my eardrums pop, but the intensity just continues to build.

Thankfully the pressure eases up the second I reach the other side. The trip through the portal takes no longer than it would to pass from one room to another. Except once I've stepped over the threshold the climate change assaults my senses in a way I never would have thought possible. Suddenly I'm standing in an entirely new world.

"This is the ship?" I ask Anne, my voice made all the more incredulous by the experience moments earlier.

Out of the gate, the hairs on my arms go as limp as my excitement.

A flat, barren landscape, pock-marked by numerous impact craters spreads out before me with all the pizazz of week-old meatloaf. Far from the high-tech starship's bridge I expected to find, it loosely reminds me of the moon. Only instead of being an ashen grey, the surface is a rusty brown. And the starry sky above has a vibrant, purple hue.

"No. This is the next enclosure," she explains. "We will need to pass through numerous enclosures if you wish to see the outer rings or the core, which comprise the bulk of this vessel."

There's that word again, "enclosure."

I notice a creature that looks somewhat like a hairless buffalo foraging in the dirt, disturbing the surface with its long snout. On closer inspection, I notice it doesn't appear to have any eyes: at least not any I can see atop its horned head.

"What is that thing?" I query.

"That is a type of slow-moving tardigrade, native to the Rigilius asteroid. Its diet consists of small insects, so it will not pose a threat to us as long as we stay out of its way," she assures me.

Incredible! I get dinosaurs, these guys get blind cows.

“I will not be able to open the next portal until my pulse emitter has fully charged, which will take approximately ten hours. You are relatively safe here for the moment,” Anne continues, “can I suggest you use this time to rest?”

Does she know I didn't sleep a wink during the night?

Probably. And while it sounds like a smart idea, my heart is still pounding. I lay down in the dirt by way of answer. I do my best to get comfortable wondering, if I do sleep, whether I still might wake up in the little bed that's back in my boring, petite apartment.

I try to fall asleep, I really do, but it's not easy given the current circumstances. Despite my exhaustion, I can't stop thinking about the supposed – and apparently quite massive – ship I'm currently inhabiting. Not to mention the construction of the asteroid my android escort expects me to doze upon. Or the blind alien cow things grazing for God-knows what kind of insects nearby. That's a heck of a lot to think about.

And what about Anne; the android who stands watch over me. She was in on it after all, just not quite the way I had initially suspected.

It's just so much to absorb.

"I have almost reached optimal charge and you have not slept," Anne points out many hours later. "Rest is essential to your wellbeing."

"I'm trying. It's just hard to stop thinking about all of this," I respond from my spot on the dusty surface. My hands, clasped behind my head as a makeshift pillow, are starting to go numb.

Anne considers my dilemma: "would engaging in sexual intercourse help you to relax?"

"WHAT?!" I almost choke as I cough the word out, sitting up with a start.

Did the robot just hit on me?!

"My databank informs me that a sexual release can have a calming effect on your species," she says casually. "Also I have noted on numerous occasions that looking at my body causes your heartbeat to increase from seventy-nine beats per minute to approximately one hundred and twenty, followed by a swelling in your..."

"Hold it right there!" I cut her off quickly. "We don't need to talk about my swelling. Let's get a couple of things straight. We are not gonna be friends and we are definitely not gonna be lovers. The only thing I want from you is your help getting off this ship. After that we go our separate ways."

Is that a look of disappointment on her face?

"Oh and I'd appreciate it if you don't offer to help me *relax* ever again," I add hastily.

"As you wish," she pouts. "My pulse emitter is now at maximum. I will open the next habitat."

I get up and brush the dust off while Anne goes through the process of opening the next doorway. Was that hurt I heard in her voice just now?

Don't be an idiot, Adam.

Projecting human emotions onto an inanimate object isn't about to get me anywhere. She's a machine you fool, and under that silky skin is probably shiny metal, battery acid and enough wiring to give an electrician nightmares. She doesn't feel things. Does she? She can't love; she can only serve. And anyway, what do I care if she does?

But as she turns my eyes instinctively glance at her rear end and I instantly hate myself for not being able to control my body's natural urges.

Dammit!

The portal appears again and my eyes strain in a vain attempt to penetrate through to the other side. I take one last gulp of asteroid air and give the weird alien cow a final glance. Anne watches curiously as I build up the courage, probably unaware how much it hurts.

Here we go again.

I step through the portal and the cold on the other side hits me like a salmon to the face. My eyes crease to slits as they attempt to beat-back the frost. A harsh wind whips off the landscape and bites into my exposed flesh. Slowed by the conditions, eventually my brain establishes what's in front of me. In fact, all around me. An endless frozen tundra.

I shiver uncontrollably and watch my breath turn to steam as I instinctively hug myself against the cold. Anne soon follows through the door and, to my annoyance, appears undisturbed by the weather.

"It's f-f-freezing in here," I state the obvious.

"We can return to the comforts of your Earth enclosure if you like?" she offers, gesturing towards the still open doorway that leads back to the asteroid belt.

"N-no. I w-won't turn back," I chatter, trying to hold my jaw still so as to not give her any further satisfaction.

"Then I had best find some shelter if you are going to survive your time here while I recharge." Anne looks off into the distance, clearly seeing further than my pathetic human eyes. "Your blood will freeze shortly."

Not gonna have any issues with swelling here.

I try to giggle at the thought, but there's no turning my mind from the cold. We begin trudging through the ankle deep slush and eventually I begin to make out fog covered mountains on the horizon. I decide to strike up a conversation to take my mind off the snow fall that is relentlessly bombarding my bare skin, chilling me to the bone.

"W-what d-did these aliens b-build this c-crazy ship f-for anyway?" I gush through vibrating teeth.

"The purpose of this craft is the preservation of life," she explains. "Each enclosure is a representation of a living world in this galaxy and contains one of every life form found here."

"L-like a g-galactic Noah's ark?" I suggest, wiping snot crystals from my nose.

"I do not know this Noah of which you speak, so I am unable to establish if that is an accurate comparison. The builders of this ship are the Preservers."

Wait, did she say one?

In the story of Noah's ark, he took two of every animal. A male and a female for obvious reasons – reproduction. How can you possibly preserve life without X and Y? If these alien "Noahs" can't breed new subjects, what do they do when one dies? Do they go kidnap a new one? I'd hate to think my escape will doom some other innocent human to a life on that rocky ledge.

*Seems like a time consuming way to preserve
life given how many creatures must exist on
this ship.*

I'm just about to pass my thoughts onto Anne when
she stops suddenly. "W-what's wrong?" I ask.

"I am detecting faint seismic activity directly beneath
us. "Perhaps we should…" Her suggestion is cut short
when a monstrous humanoid bursts out of the snow
and rakes her across the face.

Taken by surprise, Anne reels backwards as the aqua-
skinned attacker presses its advantage. Grabbing her
by both wrists it begins headbutting her repeatedly.

I stand frozen to the spot, almost literally, watching as
the alien beats up on the android. It suddenly dawns
on me that, with her hands pinned, Anne is unable to
use her laser cannon to defend herself.

I have to do something!

A surge of adrenalin sparks my legs into action. I
run up and leap onto the monster's back, wrapping
my arms around its throat and squeezing with all my
might. The steam gushing from my lungs clouds my
vision for a moment, but when it clears the truth hits
so hard I almost soil my loincloth.

Unfortunately my efforts have done little to halt its
attack on Anne. The beast's muscles are as taut as
steel cables and its neck is so thick I can barely reach
the entire way around.

Shrugging me off its back with casual ease, the beast slams Anne down so hard it makes the ice beneath them crack. The sound is enough to give the beast slight pause, and that's when I decide to try something completely stupid.

Out of sheer desperation, I scoop up a snowball and throw it hard, hitting the beast square in the back of its head. Finally the beast turns, its attention drawn away from Anne and towards me. The look in its eyes breaks the communication barrier in an instant.

Uh oh...

As its furious gaze bares down on me I realise I hadn't thought beyond getting the attacker's attention. Its steps are long and purposeful and it closes the distance between us in a heartbeat.

It utters something I don't understand in a gurgling, guttural voice then grabs me by the throat and begins to squeeze with unnatural strength. I lash out with arms and legs, but can't even make contact. Panic rises like a tidal wave as the pressure builds and my eyes bulge. The beast opens its mouth as if to roar, or to bite.

Is it going to try and eat me too?!

I'm on the verge of blacking out to that terrifying thought when I see two beautiful, feminine hands appear over the alien's broad shoulders. Anne twists the beast's head sharply to the right and with a satisfying crack, the threat is over.

The alien drops limp to the ground, and I fall with it. Pushing its hands off my throat I slowly draw in a breath of cold air like I'm trying to suck oxygen through a squished straw. Two, three, four painful wheezes and I roll to my knees. I cough a little blood as I gasp for a new round of oxygen and it stains the white snow.

"Have you sustained damage," Anne asks in that same, unaffected voice, helping me to my feet.

I rub my neck and give it a little turn left and right. A wave of dizziness threatens to topple me.

Damn that hurts!

"I-I'll be alright," I manage. I look up at my saviour and I'm immediately taken aback. "How 'bout you? You gonna be ok?" I rasp, pointing at the gash in her face. My eyes widen as I look more closely and see the strange translucent jaw bone beneath the split flesh.

That's not what I expected at all.

"My synthetic flesh will regenerate," she assures me without concern.

I slowly pull my eyes away from her wound, unwilling to ask any more questions for fear of the answers. I take a moment to examine the limp alien corpse in the snow. In the post combat calm, I can see it's actually wearing some sort of suit.

It has four obsidian black eyes, two rows of serrated teeth and small tentacles extending from the back of its skull. I notice it has a marking on its brow, just like the one I do. Instinctively my middle digit gives my own brow a rub and as my fingers run across the X it feels almost cathartic.

Another prisoner.

But its mark looks like a lightning bolt with a small circle on each side. The body suit it wears suggests a certain level of intelligence: it must have made the garment by hand. It appears to be comprised of large crustacean shells stuck to what looks like a wetsuit made of whale skin.

"W-what is it?" I ask nervously as Anne kneels down beside the creature.

"It is a Kréken from the Krés cluster," she responds. "An amphibious warrior race. This particular specimen was under the mistaken impression that you were responsible for its incarceration and was demanding you free him."

So that was what it was babbling about before it tried to choke the life out of me.

"H-how did it know this w-wasn't really... K-Krés," I inquire, sounding out the new word carefully?

"Kréken have remarkable eyesight and are able to see in light spectrums that are invisible to most other species," she theorises. "It is highly probable this ability allowed it to somehow see through the facade.

I look vainly about the frozen wasteland for a moment for any other signs of life, but then remember only one of each species is abducted. I realise this poor creature has suffered the same kind of hell as me. A shiver runs through my spine and I remember the warmth of our cave behind the waterfall. Dozing there on my little bed; served a roasted meal every night.

Or maybe it suffered even worse than me.

Thoughts begin swarming into my mind. Did this alien have its own android protector, too? And if so, would his super eyeballs allow him to see through that facade as well?

I'm about to ask the question when I'm distracted by Anne's next surprising move. "W-what are you d-doing?" I ask with concern as Anne begins to strip the Kréken's body.

"Getting you something to wear. This species is also quite adept at fashioning clothing that is resistant to the cold," Anne points out as she extracts the last limb from its suit.

And I thought it was ugly on the outside…

IV

The Kréken armour is annoying for three very good reasons. It smells like seaweed. It chafes in all the wrong places. And the huge red shells plastered all over it are heavy to lug around. But as promised by Anne, it is also incredibly warm.

So faced with wearing the cumbersome armour or catching hypothermia, I make the smart choice and keep my grumbling to myself. However, lugging this heavy outfit all the way to those distant hills is certainly off the cards. I briefly consider the prospect of curling up in a ball and waiting it all out, but a quick glance at the alien sky confirms that the conditions are deteriorating quickly.

So what's our next move?

Examining the hole from which the alien leapt in ambush, Anne discovers a tunnel leading deep underground. Light seems to bounce in from above through the ice, welcoming us in with a bright, bluish glow. Following the tunnel down, it eventually opens up into a large chamber full of old bones and animal remains. I take in the grisly scene.

This must be where it lived. This could've been where my bones wound up.

I'm almost ready to write the whole Kréken species off as a bunch of barbaric savages when something happens causing me to view them in a new light.

I catch sight of a series of markings on the icy wall that are too uniform to be random. Realising the scratches are part of some alien language, I ask Anne to translate them for.

"By the sacred bones of my ancestors, I will escape," she responds.

Her words bounce off the walls and each loop rattles me to the core. A darkness emerges in the pit of my stomach and I instinctively step back from Anne.
I think of the corpse above, now covered in snow.
Naked and alone.

He was just like me. He just wanted to go home. And now he's dead.

I spend the remainder of my time quietly contemplating this fact and wondering what else the alien and I might've had in common. If only we could have talked, maybe we could have worked together.

Maybe the enemy of my enemy could have been my friend.

When we finally do cross through the portal into the next enclosure, it's considerably warmer than the Krés habitat. Sweat begins to pool in my nether regions almost instantly. If that wasn't enough incentive to strip back to my beloved loincloth, there was also the smell, intensifying rapidly in the humidity.

Plus the suit is a constant reminder of a sentient being who had to die so that I could have it. I touch my throat, still smarting from the encounter, but mourning its outcome.

It was you or him.

"I'm going to take this lobster suit off," I say, wrinkling my nose in disgust. "It stinks of fish."

"I recommend you keep it on. The Arganon habitat has numerous large predators and that armour should provide some protection if you are attacked unexpectedly," Anne points out.

I consider ignoring her suggestion, but only for a second. A memory of raptor teeth baring through the ferns flashes across my mind and suddenly the smell of fish doesn't seem so bad. It's enough to give me second thoughts at least.

"Fine," I declare with mock resignation. "I'll keep it on, but I need to find something to get my mind off this horrible stench."

And the dead prisoner.

I focus on my new surroundings. The forest I now find myself in is full of tall, straight trees similar to those found on Earth with one noticeable difference. Their leaves are all varying shades of blue. And when I look up, I see that the sky above is an emerald green. It looks as if some cosmic deity decided to reverse the colour palette when creating this strange new world.

Endless bird calls flood out of the trees and fill the air, and after a few moments I realise it's actually all quite beautiful. Peaceful even. After the barren asteroid and frozen wasteland, a sudden desire to explore rises through my body, bringing with it excitement. But as we begin to move, the cheery chirps are replaced by a new sound.

Galloping hooves?

It comes steadily closer and I suddenly realise I've latched onto Anne's arm like a child clasping onto its mother for protection. My eyes dart about.

"What is it?" I whisper, but Anne is as still and silent as an obelisk, eyes trying to pierce through the foliage.

Does she have some sort of super vision too? Like the Kréken.

Before too long I catch my first sight of the mysterious creature causing the ruckus. An oddly coloured horse with four long antlers jutting from its skull at odd angles. Noticing our presence, the bizarre creature stops to regard us with equal parts curiosity and fear. I can guess what it is thinking:

Are these people friend or foe?

As if in answer of the unasked question the animal's mottled green fur starts to bristle nervously. It has decided we're a threat. But why, I wonder. I'm just an average guy with an X on his forehead, and she's just a super-powered android. What's to fear exactly?

It prepares to turn tail and run, so I decide to act. "It's ok, buddy. We're not here to hurt you," I assure the skittish beast.

It's about time I made a new friend.

The beast pauses at the sound of my voice. It's so beautiful and peaceful I can't help but smile. Anne and I both step forward slowly.

"What's it called?" I whisper to Anne, hoping it might respond to a familiar word.

"Arganon quadruped five-five-two-one specimen five thousand and four," she returns evenly.

What?

Seeing the confusion on my face, Anne continues while the creature watches on with trepidation. "It has no name. There are no civilized lifeforms on Arganon, therefore nobody to name it. The Preservers communicate telepathically so pronunciations only confuse the matter. A simple data entry suffices."

Simple?

"All life deserves a name," I argue. We're quite close now and I attempt to quiet my own nerves by thinking up a name. My mind shoots a few blanks instead.

C'mon Adam, how often does someone get to discover and name a new species?

We're right up by its side, its exotic smell stuffing itself right up my nose, when the answer appears out of nowhere. "There, there little Arganorse."

He seems to like it.

Anne cocks an eye in doubt at the name, then slowly reaches towards it. For a moment it seems like she is preparing to pat the majestic quadruped. Her real intention becomes dreadfully clear when a beam of energy bursts from her palm, spooking the birds above and sending them screeching into the sky. The discharge strikes the creature square between the eyes and causes its lifeless body to slump straight to the ground. A wispy trail of smoke rises from the hole in its brain.

"What the hell?!" I yell, turning on her.

There goes beautiful and peaceful.

"We both need to eat," she replies impassively.

Both? I thought she was a machine?

"But can't we eat something that wants to eat us," I fumble. "Aren't you supposed to be preserving life?

Yet you just killed the only one of those weird horse-reindeer-moose things you have on this ship."

"The Arganorse," Anne reminds me, unmoved. "And one will be back in this enclosure before too long. For now, I must stick to my primary objective, and changes in your body mass indicate a need to eat."

I let the shock ride out of my body with a shiver. I prepare a retort, something about the value of life, but I can't argue with her logic in the end. Or my grumbling stomach. There was plenty to drink on Krés, but I haven't had a proper meal since the Earth habitat and this almost getting eaten nonsense makes you hungry.

I could eat a horse... even an alien one.

"Why do you need to eat?" I ask curiously after my heartbeat returns to normal. "I mean, I understand you doing it when you were pretending to be a human, but why bother now?"

"While it is true I do not require nourishment to power my motor functions, I do need to consume organic matter in order to repair damage to my synthetic flesh," she explains, drawing my attention back to the torn skin on her face.

From what I can see through the wound on her cheek, Anne is far more complex than anything I could possibly comprehend. Before she got hurt I imagined that underneath her fleshy facade she was like the B-grade sci-fi robots I'd seen in the movies. But her bones don't appear to be metallic, or comprised of bolts and gears. They look smooth and semi-transparent, like cloudy glass or an uncut diamond.

She's even beautiful on the inside.

It begs the question: how advanced must the beings who created such a sophisticated machine be? Not to mention a spaceship large enough to house entire worlds? And what will these Preservers do if they catch me trying to escape?

Probably ditch me and abduct someone else.

I wake up on my warm, king-sized bed, groggy and confused. My face is half buried in a pillow moist with drool. I can see my alarm clock flashing the time, bathing my face periodically in its green neon light: twelve-zero-zero it claims. But it has to be well past midnight. It must have been reset by a power outage during the night.

I lay for a second trying to collect my thoughts. It's still dark out I realise. And the only sound breaking the predawn silence is the white noise coming from the static on my television.

The events from the day before dart through my mind. Putting in a gruelling fourteen hour shift at the station. Arguing with my captain. The car ride home. Turning the TV on in my bedroom. And then nothing. I must have been so exhausted I just passed out on top of the covers, still wearing my civvies.

My mouth is dry, so I decide to get a glass of water from the kitchen and that's when I realise I can't move my arms or legs. Panic stricken, I command my limbs to obey, but they remain stubbornly paralysed. All that moves is my eyes, widening in horror. I try to scream, but nothing escapes but croaky, raspy blasts of air.

Suddenly my room is alive with light and sound. It's so bright my eyes hurt and somewhere behind it a deep thrumming beat that resonates like a jackhammer deep into my bones. I feel myself moving, but not of my own accord. An invisible force lifts me up and twists me until I'm facing the door. It's open and I can see the brilliant light bursting through from outside.

From within the blinding brilliance I see movement. Three misshapen silhouettes, their heads too large and their limbs too long. I can't move. I can't cry out. I am completely at the mercy of these shadowy beings and the gut wrenching terror that recognition unlocks is like nothing I've felt before.

I start to float towards them, my world dissolving into nothing but light and the sound of my own voice. Screaming. Trapped and echoing, inside my head.

I rouse from slumber, covered in sweat to find Anne gently shaking me awake.

"What happened?" I ask her.

There's the hint of concern in her voice as she replies. "After we ate you fell asleep. Were you dreaming?"

I remember now. We entered the Arganon habitat and made camp. We ate poor Arganorse – which wasn't half as bad as I thought it would be – and then I leaned up against a tree and got comfy. I guess after two days without sleep, I was finally exhausted enough to drift off despite all the craziness.

"How long was I out?" I yawn.

"Nine hours, twenty minutes and thirty-three seconds," she says. "I apologise for waking you, but you appeared to be in distress."

"I was having a nightmare. Or maybe it was a memory. I'm not really sure," I explain.

Night had fallen and everything was bathed in the eerie violet glow given off by our campfire. I remember Anne explaining the night before that fire burns purple on this strange world due to the high levels of potassium chloride in the wood. I listen to the crackle of the kindling and lose myself peacefully in the coals for a moment before my eyes begin to wander.

Suddenly I realise I'm staring again: Anne looks beautiful in the strange light. As she turns, I notice her earlier facial wound is almost completely gone. In fact, if I didn't know about it, I would never have guessed she had been injured in the first place.

Wow, she heals fast.

I move my head from side to side and it's still stiff. I can feel the bruises around my neck, no doubt in the perfect shape of a Kréken's digits.

Me, not so much.

I sit quietly for a while watching the flames flicker – watching her – and pondering whether my dream was really fact or fiction. It felt real, but if it did happen, how could I have possibly forgotten it? Unless it was so traumatic I repressed the memories.

Or I was made to forget.

"Anne, why did your makers choose me?" I question, breaking the silence.

"They needed a healthy, fully grown homo sapien to add to their collection," she replies instantly. "Beyond that I have no additional information to provide on why you specifically were chosen."

"I swear I won't let them take me again. I'd rather die," I tell her, searching for a reaction.

"I will do everything in my power to prevent that from happening," she assures me.

That actually makes me smile. I may be heading into the unknown, but with Anne and her laser canon by my side, I'm confident I can overcome anything these aliens can throw at me.

Assuming she really is on my side, of course?

V

Travelling through an alien space zoo, you learn to expect the unexpected. You accept that you are going to see things you don't understand and experience a truckload of stuff that's downright incomprehensible. But you also take comfort in the small things; the universal truths.

Despite how alien and foreign the habitats may seem at first glance, they contain much that is still familiar. Grass still grows from the ground. Snow still falls from the heavens. The winds still blow delicious oxygen and the sun – or suns as the case may be – shine light down upon the surface. And if something has sharp teeth, it will probably try and eat you.

I think it's these truths that make the fifth habitat so very disturbing. The complete and utter lack of familiarity. No ground. No sky. No comforting pull of gravity to help orient yourself. Just white, luminous nothingness in all directions.

"What the hell kind of planet is this?" I ask as I acclimate poorly to the new feeling of weightlessness. I clutch at my stomach as if that will hold back the wave of vertigo threatening to empty Arganorse right out of my stomach.

"None that I have on record," she replies, grabbing a hold of my arm, then interlocking our fingers to prevent us from floating apart. "It appears we have entered an unused enclosure, possibly for a future habitat yet to be assigned."

"It reminds me of the hyperbolic time chamber," I muse as we float through the void, hand in hand.

"I am unfamiliar with that location. What purpose does it serve?"

"It's not a real place," I chuckle. "It's something from this anime I used to watch when I was a kid. Maybe when we get back to Earth we'll watch it together. I think you'd like it. It even has androids in it."

"It was my understanding that we would be parting company once you were free of this vessel. Your exact words were: 'the only thing I want from you is your help getting off this ship. After that we are going our separate ways.'"

> I sound like a giant ass when she puts it like that.

"Oh right," I murmur sheepishly. "Look, about that. I didn't mean all those things I said earlier. I was a little overwhelmed and I may have taken it out on you. I see now none of this is actually your fault and I'm sorry if I hurt your feelings."

"Your apology is unnecessary, Adam. I do not have any feelings to hurt," she replies.

Ok, I'm definitely an ass.

"Well that's good then, I guess." My response is unable to soften the awkwardness. I quickly turn my attention back to the endless white. "So what are we going to do here for the next ten hours?"

"I'm sure I can find some way to keep you entertained," Anne prompts.

"You're not going all sexbot on me again are you?" I tease, arching an eyebrow.

"No," she quickly injects. "You made your feelings quite clear on that subject. Your exact words were..."

"Yeah, yeah. I remember," I cut in. "So what did you have in mind?"

"According to my databank, playing games are a popular way of passing time on Earth," she says, looking for confirmation on my face. "I was going to suggest we do that?"

XXXX

After an unsuccessful attempt at eye-spy, a thumb war that almost cost me an appendage and numerous games of rock-paper-scissors – during which Anne kept questioning the logic of paper defeating rock – I finally give up.

I rub at my forehead in frustration and consider what to do next. Tentatively I suggest she should pick a game to play.

This should be good…

"I am programmed with a wide selection of classic Earth games. Are you familiar with chess?" she asks, a hologram appearing above her palm.

I stare open-mouthed at the projection of a chess board, complete with pieces, floating in the air between us.

"That's amazing," I gape. "Why didn't you tell me you could do that before?"

"You never asked me to select a game before now," she responds matter-of-factly.

I cast an eye of suspicion over her placid face. Anne may be incapable of telling a direct lie, but I've noticed she has absolutely no problem omitting a thing or two when she chooses.

"Anything else you failed to mention?" I begin, my brain running through the possibilities. "Can you fly? Shape shift? Or are you fluent in over six million forms of communication?"

"I cannot fly or change my form, and according to my database that many languages do not currently exist," she begins to explain.

Oh, well. I guess a flying android was too much to hope for.

"I speak one hundred thousand, three hundred and twenty two languages, but I am capable of learning more if you can provide samples of the other five million, eight hundred thousand, six hundred and seventy eight."

Sarcasm; clearly not her strong suit.

"I can also simulate all human functions except for that of reproduction," Anne continues. "I can regenerate my synthetic flesh as you have already seen. I can shoot lasers from the beam emitter in my right palm and I can also create three-dimensional holograms of anything contained within my databank using the projector in my left."

"I can also open portals across short distances and through all five dimensions using the pulse emitter that is located inside my head," she adds.

"Got it," I nod as if knowingly, but in turth I'm barely able to take it all in.

Five what?

Wait, anything in her database: I begin thinking out loud, "so can you show me a hologram of this ship?"

"Of course," she replies nonchalantly, changing the board game into two concentric rings spinning around a small central sphere.

"What am I looking at exactly?" I quiz her.

"This is the outer ring," Anne explains pointing at the largest ring. "This is where the drop pods are located and where we need to go in order to leave the ship."

"This location here," she pauses, indicating the slightly smaller ring within, "is observation. We must avoid going here. This is where the Preservers watch over the specimens they have collected."

"Specimens like me," I interrupt. "Do they know I've left my enclosure?"

"There are many habitats and even more inhabitants. It's unlikely your absence has been noticed," she assures me.

Yet...

"This is the core," she says, pointing through the hologram to its centre. "Everything from propulsion to life support is controlled from within this sphere by a series of automatons."

"So where are the enclosures?" I ask, eyeing the map for any indication.

"This is where the artificial habitats exist," she answers, indicating all the empty space between the rings and the central sphere.

"I don't get it," I say, studying the hologram. "Where are the borders that separate them?"

"The enclosures inhabit the same space and time, with each one encapsulated within its own pocket dimension," Anne reveals. "This ship is in a state of quantum flux, existing across multiple dimensions at the same time. This allows the Preservers access to infinite storage space within the confines of a single vessel. I will attempt to clarify. The first law of five-dimensional physics states..."

"Long story short," I cut her off, "it's bigger on the inside then the outside. Doesn't look like a phone box from the outside does it?" I joke.

"I do not understand the question," Anne prompts, perhaps hoping for more information.

"Forget it," I shut her down, a smirk revealing my moment of self-appreciation. I run my eyes over the hologram, soaking it all in. "I'm still not clear about one thing though. If these habitats all exist on top of one another, why do we have to travel through each one to get to the outer ring? Can't you just open a door straight to the drop pods?"

Anne thinks for a second before answering: "I can, but the portals are altering your quantum frequency ever so slightly each time you pass through one. That is the small pressure you feel in your head when you enter. Done slowly the damage is minimal, but move too quickly through the frequencies and the resulting pressure could become extremely unpleasant for you."

That's ominous.

"How unpleasant are we talking, here?" I ask.

"Your skull could explode," she replies, disturbingly deadpan as usual.

I cross my arms discouraged. "That's pretty unpleasant. Let's not do that."

VI

After what feels like an eternity, Anne announces that her pulse emitter is finally fully charged and ready to whisk us away to our next locale. I am keen to put everything about this horrid white enclosure behind me, including a zero gravity bathroom incident I made Anne swear to never speak of again.

Thank god she doesn't have a sense of humour. Anyone else who saw that would still be laughing.

Alive and mostly dry, I wait out the last few minutes with eager anticipation. "How do you decide where the portal opens up?" I query, the question suddenly popping into my head. "What part of the enclosure?"

"These portals allow travel through five-dimensional space," Anne starts. "So they open in the exact same spot each time, but in the next dimension."

"So you can't ensure the portal opens somewhere safe?" I ask with trepidation.

"I have no idea what is on the other side Adam. When it comes to my primary objective, travelling through these enclosures are not my desired course of action," Anne confirms, her point crystal clear.

Some of my enthusiasm for getting out of this strange habitat extinguished, I'm still convinced there is no turning back. When the newly opened portal appears, I take a deep breath and leap through.

It's quite a shock feeling the tug of gravity again after being weightless for so long. It's even more of a shock to find myself plunging feet first into freezing cold water. But the greatest shock of all is when I start to sink deeper and deeper into the icy depths and suddenly remember...

Crap, I can't swim!

I begin to splash about pathetically as panic takes hold. Somehow, my uncoordinated flailing gets me to the surface long enough to see the doorway hovering above. It's still open, yet agonisingly out of reach. I begin to sink again into the vast blue sea taking a gulp of air with me for the ride.

Where the hell could Anne possibly be? This is the end!

I claw helplessly at the surrounding water, which simply ignores me, bending around my fingers where I needed it to somehow latch on. Bubbles begin streaming from my nose and mouth, my lungs burning as the last of my precious oxygen leaves for greener pastures. I fight my natural instinct to draw another breathe, but it's a losing battle.

Finally, this is it.

A peace settles over me and I stop clawing. I'm about to give in and let the water take me when the most miraculous thing happens. I feel a strong grip around my waist pulling me upwards to safety. With it, the last echoes of breath fly from my body.

When I finally breakthrough the surface I heave down a lungful of oxygen greedily while Anne's strong arms keep my head above water.

"I can't swim," I cough and splutter!

"Yes. I gathered that," she notes.

Maybe she can do sarcasm after all.

"Calm down; I have you now. But I must warn you; the waters of Oce'ana are full of large predators. Your splashing is going to draw their attention."

Her words don't help. My heart already racing, I begin to look about in all directions as Anne keeps us afloat with unnatural buoyancy. All I can see is water: there's no land anywhere. And then, I go completely still.

Oh bloody hell!

"Anne," I yelp like a wounded seal. "Something's touching my leg."

That something coils its way around my ankle before Anne has a chance to reply. It pulls down with ungodly strength and before I know it I'm back under water having a killer case of déjà vu.

The undersea life of Oce'ana is truly a wonder to behold. Schools of multi-coloured tropical fish swim about searching for food with one eye, while watching out for predators with the other. I witness a quick-witted cephalopod-looking creature use a blast of ink to escape a hungry beast with rows of teeth so sharp they would make a shark green with envy.

I'm sure I would find the scene totally fascinating if it were one of those late-night documentaries and I was sitting safe and sound on my couch at home. But unfortunately, it isn't and I'm not. And there's the small issue of my impending death.

This will be the last thing I ever see. At least it was interesting.

The tentacle that has my leg continues to drag me downwards. I kick uselessly at it with my free foot. To her credit, Anne refuses to let go, holding onto my other hand so tight it feels like she might break my bones. My shoulder is definitely starting to displace, but it's the least of my worries.

I'm sure she could use that strength to break me free if she could just get her hands on whatever has my ankle. But it's dragging me to my doom so fast she can only be pulled along for the ride.

Finally I get a glance at my captor. Down below I see an enormous mountain of rainbow hued coral with a gaping black maw in the middle so big it could swallow a Volkswagen whole. The mouth is surrounded by long white protrusions and I suddenly realise what I thought was a tentacle is actually a tongue pulling me straight down. Straight down its gullet.

This is it. Eaten.

Even if Anne freed me right now, I'd drown before we could ever reach the surface. Resigned to my fate, I close my eyes and allow myself to be pulled down the monster's throat.

XXXX

Upon entering the maw the protrusions – which I can only assume are teeth – close forming a perfect seal. The water starts to drain forcing us to follow it down the oesophagus. We ride the grotesque water slide through a series of twists and turns until finally we are dropped into an enormous gastric chamber. We splash into the floor, which is covered in six-inches of luminescent yellow fluid.

I'm not dead.

Water gushes out my nose and mouth, bringing snot and vomit up with it. With each heave I can feel the bruises around my neck pulse in pain. Crawling through the goo, I take a few deep breaths of the foul smelling air, grateful to be alive after such an ordeal.

“Get up!” Anne orders, leaping to her feet.

“Why? What’s going on?” I wheeze, trying and failing to stand. Realising I’m too weak to support myself after what I’ve just endured, Anne scoops me up as if I weigh nothing.

“I recommend keeping out of the Anthodaria’s stomach acid if you are going to survive your time here,” she explains, once I’m safely up in her arms and out of harm’s way.

Through the sickly yellow glow I see the fumes wafting lazily up from my hands and knees, right where they were submerged in the digestive fluids only moments ago. I’m suddenly thankful I decided to keep wearing the rubbery Kréken bodysuit that covers me from neck to toe. It is the only thing that kept my flesh from coming into direct contact with the caustic substance.

“You’re still standing in that stuff,” I point out. “Are you going to be alright?”

Anne look down for the briefest of instants. “The acid will dissolve the synthetic flesh around my feet, but my skeletal structure will hold. We should remain quite safe here until my pulse emitter is fully charged.”

Safe? Here?

I’m not really sure why I start to laugh at that moment. Maybe it’s her use of the word “safe,” given we’re in the belly of giant coral monster at the bottom of an alien ocean. Maybe it’s the way she now cradles me like a helpless baby. Or a bizarre parody of a groom carrying his bride over the threshold.

Or maybe I've finally lost my mind.

Whatever the reason, I laugh long and hard until the sound blends with the sounds of metabolic breakdown and gastric emissions.

VII

In the near darkness and relaxed in Anne's arms, I sleep like a baby. When she finally wakes me, it's so we can leave Oce'ana. I wipe drool from my lip and try to shake out the cobwebs, grudgingly admitting to myself it was the best rest I've had in weeks.

Feeling extremely emasculated after being carried around by my five-foot-eight companion, I eagerly hop out of her arms. Careful not to touch the lake of horror nestled around her feet, I leap straight through the sixth doorway.

As with the previous jumps, I'm surprised by what I find on the other side as I try to lock my feet onto the hard, unnatural ground without stumbling. The first shock is aural, the sudden change from the intestinal soundtrack of my previous cnidarian prison to this environment jarring. But that's the least of my worries.

I appear to be in a circular metal corridor. It reminds me of a subway tunnel, except instead of a platform on one side, it has a series of large, transparent tubes. The tubes reach from floor to ceiling, and each contains an alien lifeform, seemingly frozen inside.

"What planet is this supposed to be?" I ask, as Anne appears behind me. "Cybertron?"

I baulk at the sight of her crystalline feet, watching as what little remains of her synthetic flesh hisses as it dissolves to gas above the cold metal floor.

"No. This is not an artificial habitat. This is the vessel's core," she reveals.

The what?!

Did she say the core! Anger surges through me like a hot wave of lava. "What the hell are you trying to pull? You were supposed to be taking me out of this ship, not deeper into it!"

"I assure you I am not pulling anything. I merely require equipment and supplies that are essential to your escape. And they can only be obtained here at the core," she explains. "Need I point out that if I wished to betray you, I could have done so numerous times by now?

"How do I know you haven't?" I throw at her before I have time to think it over.

"You may need to cross quantum fields slowly, but I have no such limitation," she replies. "If I wanted I could take a portal straight to the inner ring and inform the Preservers of your plans."

My anger fades in the face of such irrefutable logic.

I really need to quit jumping to conclusions.

"You're right," I settle the argument. "I'm sorry."

"As I have stated previously, your apologies are unnecessary, but your compliance is," Anne commands. "I require you to wait here while I acquire the tools we need."

"Why can't I come with you?" I ask.

Geez, now I sound like a child, too.

"The area I need to enter is controlled by automatons who are not programmed to preserve your existence as I am," she says. "You will be much safer if you wait here in cryogenics."

"How long will you be?" I query.

Anne barely thinks it over: "I estimate the task will take me one hour and three minutes. Do you promise to remain here until I return?"

"Scout's honour," I beam, one hand on my heart and the other raised in mock salute.

"I have no scouts in my database and I'm unable to confirm if they have honour," she frowns.

"I'll stay in cryogenics," I sigh. "Now go do what you gotta do." I clarify this point by shooing her away with my hands.

As she leaves I hear the clunk of her footsteps and glance again down at her feet. The sparkling "bone" beneath makes it look like she is wearing a pair of expensive diamond slippers. When she disappears around the bend I turn my attention back to the tubes and the fascinating contents within.

What to do?

I promised I'd stay in cryogenics, but I didn't say where in cryogenics. I smile slyly to myself, strolling away in the opposite direction.

XXXX

The cryo-tubes contain creatures of every conceivable shape, colour and size. From tiny reptilian humanoids to man-sized molluscs. Moving from one to the next I can't help but marvel at the sheer amount of life that exists in the galaxy.

Those NASA eggheads have spent the last fifty years searching the cosmos for proof of alien life and here I am with evidence of it all around me and no way of proving it.

What I wouldn't give for a camera right now.

Not everything I find is foreign, however. Peering into the tubes I occasionally stumble across something familiar. From one pod a black cat with bright yellow eyes stares out at me, frozen in time.

Further on I find one of those tardigrade things from the asteroid habitat. Then a blue skinned Kréken like the one that looks exactly like the one that attacked me. Then…

Oh God.

My heart drops like an untethered anchor as my galactic sightseeing tour comes to an abrupt end. Floating lifelessly in the tube before me I see a human male. Eyes closed as if sleeping and naked as the day he was born. What poor family currently wonders what happened to their son? The question rages at me, boiling my blood.

Wait a second. He looks familiar, I think I know…

I lean in closer, then closer again. Then I leap back in horror. I gasp in shock and the sharp sound rattles off down the corridor. My legs go suddenly weak and I stumble to the floor, before sliding my butt back further until I hit the opposite wall. My gaze never leaves the horrible tube.

He looks just like me.

As if finding a man in cryogenic suspension wasn't disturbing enough, discovering it's some sort of ancestor is just horrendous.

Is this the textbook definition of surreal?

Slowly I get back to my feet and creep closer again, nervously this time. Face eventually pushed up against the tube, my eyes try to pierce through the frozen fluid.

We aren't completely identical. His forehead hasn't been branded with a cross like mine, for starters. He's bulkier, too. I feel sick.

What does it mean?

I clutch at the tightness I feel growing across my chest. Anxiety? I'm starting to panic. Something is not right. I begin rubbing at my X uncontrollably. Furiously.

How is this possible?

"You said you would wait for me," Anne says, startling me almost as much as my cryo-twin. Then I grab her, more violently than I intend.

"I want answers! Tell me who the hell that is right now?!" I demand.

"It's Adam Furst," she answers without hesitation.

"No God dammit, I'm Adam Furst!" I scream in disbelief. I try to shake her as if to loosen some other truth, but I can't shift her a millimetre and she just stares back at me unmoved, literally and figuratively.

"Adam Furst, the human being from whom you were cloned," she says casually, as if we were discussing the weather.

She's telling the truth, I can feel it.

I slowly let go of her, barely hearing her continued explanation as I search for some evidence to the contrary. "The Preservers keep the original specimens here so they can use their DNA to clone replacement subjects whenever one perishes."

What the hell?

"No. That can't be true... I remember my life," I counter, but it is whisper weak.

"The host memories are transferred through a process we call memory stamping," she replies calmly, seemingly shrugging it all off.

Oh yeah, sure; fine. No big deal.

"This is bullshit!" is all I can offer in argument.

From my vantage point slightly below the other Adam I have a clear view of his chin. Something catches my eye; a faint scar. I remember how I got it. I fell off my bike when I was ten and had to get three stitches just under my jaw. My mates thought it was cool, and when I was a bit older I would tell girls I got it in a fight to try and impress them.

I touch my own chin, but no matter how much I feel around I can't feel any evidence of a wound ever existing there. I can remember how it felt to run your finger over it, too: the slight bump just under the bone.

I can remember it, damn it!

But now, nothing. I race over to a reflective panel in a nearby wall and stare at the person looking back at me as if for the first time. A face in shock. Dirtied, bloodied, bearded, but familiar. I lift my chin, and notice a bit of bruising rising up from under the Kréken's suit where its previous owner had tried to strangle me – but there's no scar.

How did I not notice?

It's true. I'm a clone. The realisation almost breaks me then and there. I begin trying to think it out and rationalise it all, but my mind is a ruin. Crumbled into bits. Is that why they don't need a male and female I wonder? Is it because they use clones to populate their habitats? But I quickly reject the idea.

The X.

I rub the letter on my forehead with newfound trepidation. "Wha... What does the X mean?" I gasp, suddenly short of breath. I already know the answer.

"That signifies that you are the tenth clone in the Adam line," Anne confirms, devastatingly.

Oh God.

I begin to sway. I feel sick and even retch once as tears well in my eyes. The anger rages through me like some unleashed demon. Anne studies my face: "May I suggest you sit down? You appear to be hyperventilating."

I'm just about to tell her where she can stick her suggestion when she lunges at me. With deft hands

Anne plunges a hypodermic needle into my neck and releases the contents with an almost peaceful *shush* sound. Before I can even register what's going on the warm liquid is spreading through my bloodstream.

She's been playing me all along!

"What... have... you... done?" I plead, the last word barely a whisper as my vision begins to blur and my legs give out.

The last thing I see is the face of my betrayer, standing over me mouthing words I can't make out. I roll my head and catch a glimpse of the real Adam Furst, before I fall into a blissful, drug induced slumber.

VIII

Time has no meaning as I drift in and out of consciousness. My fevered dreams blur into reality, then back again: my mind unable to differentiate between the two. I find myself being chased through long city streets by a crowd of killer robots that all share my face.

This can't be real.

But I run anyway. Then I'm floating in a tub of cold water fully clothed. I tell myself it's a dream, but the waterlogged feeling in my ears screams otherwise. Then suddenly I'm trapped inside an Egyptian pyramid infested with scarabs who dig their way into my flesh. I know it can't be true.

But the crawling sensation beneath my skin feels all too real.

Eventually the discomfort ceases and I find myself floating peacefully through the dark reaches of space surrounded by millions of twinkling stars.

For all I know this is the truth. Maybe after she drugged me, Anne shoved me out an airlock. Is this finally it?

There is only one constant throughout this series of random, disjointed events. Anne's disembodied voice assuring me everything will be ok. She's holding me now, and everything will be fine.

Yeah, right!

Eventually my fever breaks and my head starts to clear. I wake to see clouds drifting lazily through an emerald green sky lit by a blazing blue sun. It seems familiar, but my eyes are struggling to focus. Then I spot the ashes of a fire.

How did I get back to the Arganon habitat?

"What happened?" I croak through parched lips.

"Much has happened while you slept," Anne replies. "You will need to be more specific."

"YOU!" I snap. Jumping to my feet, I point an accusing finger at her face. "What the hell did you do to me?!"

"I did many things to you. You will need to be..."

"THE NEEDLE! What the hell was in the needle Anne?!" I scream, rubbing the spot on my neck where she stuck me.

Anne produces a calming motion with her hands in response: "the injection I gave you contained millions of microscopic nanites."

Not the answer I was expecting.

"Nanites? Like tiny machines?" I produce, caught completely off guard.

"Exactly like tiny machines," she replies. "These particular nanites have been programmed to repair the damage you have sustained during the many trips we have taken through the portals."

"What damage?" I ask. "You said if we go slowly there wouldn't be any damage."

"No. I said the damage would be minimal," she corrects me. "Without the nanites you would have eventually succumbed to radiation poisoning. Your life expectancy had diminished to approximately two Earth years by the time I injected you. But thanks to the nanites now residing in your bloodstream, your body is able to purge any damage caused by the radiation."

That's actually kind of awesome.

"Well you could've told me all that before jabbing me with a needle," I grumble suspiciously, my anger starting to ebb. "So, how long was I out?"

"Three days," she retorts.

"THREE DAYS?!" I repeat flabbergasted.

"Yes. The nanites took considerably longer to repair the initial damage than I predicted," she says, casually stoking at a new flame that is growing into life, reaching up eagerly from the fire pit. "You will be pleased to know I continued our journey while you were out, albeit at a slightly slower pace. I even liberated some clothing and supplies I thought you might appreciate."

I look down for the first time and realise I've changed. With all the accusations and explanations flying around I completely failed to notice I was no longer wearing the smelly Kréken armour or the revealing loincloth. Both had been replaced by a pair of sneakers, denim jeans and a grey leather jacket over a black t-shirt. The very same clothes I fell asleep in the night I was abducted, I realise.

No, that wasn't me. That was the real Adam Furst. I'm nothing but an alien's science project. A cheap, broken copy with a head full of false memories.

"What about your speech on staying protected from predators," I query, trying not to think of Anne changing me like a toddler in my sleep.

"Your fever was too high for the suit and these are the exact right size. Allow me to show you what else I have acquired," she follows, trying to distract me further from my angst. Not that she can.

What am I even fighting to escape for? The real me is in a tube. I'm the tenth. The tenth. There will be an eleventh. There will probably be a hundred more just like me!

As she closes the distance between us I notice I'm not the only one who has had an interesting wardrobe change. Anne now wears a nondescript black bodysuit with a brown belt and two gun-like devices strapped to her hips. They remind me of a pistol. Her feet also appear mended.

I wonder what she killed this time.

She reaches out and raises my left hand, and I let her do as she will. She tries to draw my attention to the black fingerless glove I now wear over it. It appears to have some sort of small screen attachment, but I have very little interest in the device at this time. Distracted, my mind is elsewhere.

I don't care.

"That is a universal translator, created by a race called the Medians," she begins explaining. "They only have three fingers, however. Luckily, I was able to find a glove from another specimen in the Depository after locating your clothes, and with some minor modifications I was able to combine the two so that you will be..."

What is she talking about? Why am I even listening? Why am I putting myself through any of this? I'm not even me. I'm number ten. Ten! They're happy for me to fail; they will just keep testing me and testing me until I crack. They're always watching. There's no hope.

"What about those?" I interrupt impatiently, pointing at the guns. "Are those for me?"

"One of them is. I felt it was necessary for you to be able to defend yourself should I become incapacitated." She removes one from its holster and hands it over. The first thing I note is how much lighter it is compared to a police issue revolver.

"Who's the other one for?" I ask.

Anne pats it as it lies against her hip: "that is for me."

"But you can shoot lasers from your hands," I point out, as I turn the gun over in my hands admiring the smooth lines and the way the light glints off the sleek silver metal. Holding the weapon, a sudden calmness settles over me like a warm blanket.

"Yes. But doing so drains a lot of power. Power that can be better used to charge my pulse emitter," she explains. "Would you like to test the weapon?"

Recalling Adam's academy training, I grip the gun with both hands and align my sight, aiming for a large stone at the edge of our camp. I gently squeeze the trigger. *Pew!* With zero recoil a bolt of red plasma springs forth and turns the rock into a pile of rubble.

"Cool." The word slowly emerges from my mouth, almost unconsciously.

"Incorrect. The energy discharge was extremely hot," the android amends.

"Figure of speech," I explain listlessly, giving her a wan smile. I pause for a moment and rub my stomach as the realisation of what I need to do materialises in my mind. I groan and hear my own voice spill into the space between us…

"Hey, I'm starving. I don't suppose you could go get me a bite to eat?" I ask.

"Of course," she replies. "I shall return shortly."

I watch Anne disappear into the woods and once I feel certain she is sufficiently out of ear shot, I utter a curse word under my breath. Pressing the cold gun barrel to my temple, I pull the trigger.

XXXX

Needless to say, I'm a little surprised to be alive seconds after attempting to shoot myself in the head. It's not how I thought it would work. Through gritted teeth I fire again. And again. But death does not come. For some reason the damn thing refuses to fire and I'm left with no option other than to fall to my knees in defeat, anguished tears streaming down my face.

I wish the ground would swallow me whole.

"The power pack is depleted," Anne explains, stepping out from her hiding spot behind a tree.

"You knew?" I sob. "That's why you gave me a gun with only one shot left in it."

"I suspected, yes. The third Adam killed himself after discovering he was clone. It was logical to assume you might try the same thing given your similarities."

"The third Adam?" I query.

"Yes. As I mentioned earlier there have been ten Adam clones in total and I have personally known eight out of those ten," she reminisces.

I rub at my forehead again. Harder this time. I can't stop, until I realise for the first time I'm crying.

I don't know how much more of this I can take.

"Eight," I repeat. "Where were you for the other two?"

"I was not built yet," Anne explains. "It was the actions of the first two Adams that necessitated my creation."

Curiosity begins to push away my tears; "what does that mean?"

"I will attempt to clarify," Anne pauses for a second. "Almost all the lifeforms in this galaxy, no matter how advanced or unique, share one common trait: a sense of self preservation. Homo sapiens, however, are one of a very select few who appear to have the ability to override this innate need to survive and choose instead to self-terminate."

"You're saying no other species in the galaxy commits suicide?" I ask her incredulously, wiping the last of my hot tears from my swollen eyes.

"Not exactly. The Preservers had observed other lifeforms sacrificing themselves in the past, but the reason for doing so was always clear to them. They could understand a lifeform sacrificing itself to protect one of its own kind – someone with whom they shared a familial bond, or even a cherished mating partner. But the cases of human self-termination baffled them," she clarifies.

They should try living life on this side of their little project!

"When the first Adam clone took his own life," Anne continues, "the Preservers simply thought it a random anomaly. But when the second one did the same thing they realised they were encountering something new and would need to adopt a more unorthodox approach if a homo sapien specimen was to survive and thrive in captivity. That is when they created me. My sole purpose, to ensure the clones of Adam were kept alive and healthy."

Although I hear everything she says, it's the words "captivity" and "specimen" that jump out at me.

They think I'm a science experiment.

As if accentuating her point she hands me a round blue fruit.

I guess it's feeding time at the zoo.

"Unfortunately I have not always been successful in this regard," she admits.

"You mean Adam three?" I ask, before taking a big bite out of the surprisingly tart fruit, causing sticky juice to dribble down my chin.

"Yes. When I first met him I started by explaining who and what I was. I explained where we were and how he came to be. He did not believe me at first, but eventually I was able to convince him my words were true. It was shortly thereafter I found him hanging from a vine he had used to block his oxygen inhalation."

Damn! I should've thought of that.

I think of the Kréken suddenly and realise now why he had no android bodyguard. He would never kill himself. He would escape or die trying.

"So is that when they told you to lie?" Even I was surprised by the anger in my voice, but if Anne picked up on it, it didn't show.

"Deception is not an area the Preservers have a lot of experience with. Being a race of telepathic beings it's challenging for them to keep secrets from one another for long, so they were ill-equipped to program me in the intricacies of lying. Their solution was to have me stay silent. That method seemed to work remarkably well. The fourth, sixth, seventh, eighth and ninth clones lived long, happy lives."

"Really? I can't imagine any version of me being happy playing Tarzan for the rest of his life," I reply speculatively. "What about Adam Five? I noticed you skipped him."

"Like you, he suspected something was amiss early on and decided to follow me into the jungle in the hopes of learning my secret," Anne explains. "I should mention most of the clones attempted this at one point or another – following me around, watching me hunt – until their suspicions were sated."

"Unfortunately," she quickly continues, "much like your attempt, the fifth Adam was attacked by a wild animal during this endeavour. I was forced to use my laser cannon to slay the predator, but not before it was able to latch onto his left forearm. I did my best to stabilise his condition, but the tiger bite caused irreparable damage. Once gangrene set in I was left with no other option than to call the Preservers for assistance."

"What happened next?" I prompt.

Why am I suddenly so interested in this?

A flicker of awareness reminds me that I was indeed hungry, and did, in fact, have food in my hand. But I now sit spellbound: morbidly curious to learn of the fate of the other me – which was almost the fate of me… or the tenth me.

Or whatever.

"I cannot be certain. The Preservers took him away and I never saw him again," she says. As if registering my dissatisfaction with that answer, Anne adds, "if I were to speculate on what happened, I would think he died of his injuries. It was not long after that the sixth Adam clone was created."

"So if I off myself they'll just keep making more Adam clones, and those clones will either die horrible deaths or live long lives ignorant of the truth?" It wasn't really a question. I had already realised what I needed to do and was filled with a new-found determination. "I need to break this cycle once and for all."

"If that is your wish I will assist you any way I can," Anne reiterates.

Taking the gun from my hands, Anne ejects the depleted clip and replaces it with a fresh power pack she plucks from her belt.

"This weapon will now fire stun bolts only," she informs me. "Shooting yourself will only result in a mild electric shock and a nasty headache."

"You don't trust me,' I accuse Anne, "but I get that. You have nothing to worry about though – I won't try to kill myself again. I give you my word."

Maybe she does really care about me.

"Good," she answers. "It would be a shame if I were forced to break your arms and legs to prevent you from harming yourself."

Maybe not.

I laugh nervously. "I guess you were programmed with a sense of humour, after all."

"I was not," she replies flatly.

IX

Wow, that's cold.

The first thing I do as I step back into the Krés enclosure is zip my jacket up until it's wedged into my chin. It's still uncomfortably chilly, but at least I won't have to risk losing my toes to frostbite like the last time I was here.

"I recommend caution," Anne says, drawing her weapon. "There will be another Kréken clone in this habitat by now."

These Preservers work fast.

"Don't worry. He won't catch me off guard this time," I reply, sounding more confident than I feel. Staring down the barrel of my gun, I swivel my head from side to side waiting for the aqua-skinned alien to leap out from his hidey hole just like it did the last time.

We both remain quiet and alert, but no threat is forthcoming. Eventually Anne suggests we should keep moving so I can stay warm and we make our way across the ice, heading nowhere in particular.

For the longest time there is nothing at all to see but my breath as it turns to mist every time I exhale.

And nothing to listen to but the rhythmic sound of footsteps crunching in the snow.

"How come it took you three days to move me only three enclosures," I inquire, trying to break the silence.

"There were complications on Oce'ana," she responds with no further elaboration. Her blank expression gives me little to go off, but I decide to return us to the sounds of crunching snow in place of further enquiry.

Best I don't know.

I begin to remember our last Kréken encounter, and realise my neck still does not feel quite right. I think about the etchings on the wall, and slowly a plan begins to take shape in my mind. I'm wondering whether to voice it to Anne when she comes to a sudden stop.

She pans the landscape, looking intently at something I can't see. "It is close."

"How do you work this universal translation thingy?" I ask, holding up the black glove and its blank screen.

"Tap the screen twice, then say the language you wish translated to begin. Tap twice a second time and say 'end' when you are done," Anne instructs.

I do as she says and the screen starts to glow green as it awaits my instructions. Bringing the device close to my lips, I speak a single word; "Kréken."

Here we go…

"We know you're out there!" I yell. The band on my wrist translates my speech into a series of gurgling, guttural sounds that I hope don't carry across any of the nerves I heard in my own voice.

"By the sacred bones of my ancestors I swear we mean you no harm!" I add. "We just want to talk!"

"Are you sure he can hear me?" I ask, putting my hand over the UT's screen to stop it repeating my words.

"I am certain. His heartbeats have increased from ninety-nine beats per minute to one hundred and eighty since you began speaking," she explains.

Nervous or angry?

"Kréken are not known for diplomacy," she continues. "The only thing they truly respect is strength. I believe we can use that to our advantage. Get ready, I have a plan. Anne holsters her weapon and sprints away before I can ask her to elaborate.

But what about my plan?

Thankfully I pick up the gist fairly quickly as she runs into the trap – it doesn't take long for our quarry to take the bait. When the Kréken finally erupts from below the surface revealing itself, I'm ready. I drop it with a well-placed stun bolt between the shoulder blades moments before it can lay a hand on Anne.

With the danger now past we reassemble around our fallen foe. As we meet over its twitching form she starts talking gobbledygook and I stare at her dumbfounded until the UT spits out, "well done, Master Adam." It takes a second, but I realise she is now speaking Kréken.

Master? What game is she playing?

"Um... thanks," I reply awkwardly.

"Yes. Well done pink-skin. You have bested me. Now finish off the job," the alien agrees groggily, its words also turned into perfect English thanks to the miraculous glove.

"Kill you?" Anne replies incredulously. "You are not worthy of being killed by one such as my Master. He who wrestled the carnivorous velociraptor of Earth and lived to tell the tale..."

Wrestled is not exactly the way I remember it, but ok.

"He who survived ten hours in a coral creature's noxious belly..."

While being carried like a baby, I might add.

"The only being in the entire galaxy to escape a Preserver prison..."

Wow! That one's kinda true.

It never occurred to me to ask whether anyone else had ever escaped their habitat. I feel a sudden surge of pride welling up inside me at the realisation that I am the only being to have achieved this feat. I cock my gun to the side in salute to my badassery.

"Shall I dispose of this lowly wretch for you, Master Adam?" she defers to me in a subservient manner.

"That won't be necessary," I play along. "I've decided to spare this one."

The alien stares up at me a moment, its four black eyes wide with shock.

"Thank you, noble warrior," it finally replies in pain, as the last jolts of electricity dancing over its muscular form finally begin to dissipate.

As Anne helps him get to his feet it says: "I am Zanatos of clan Nyx. My life now belongs to you as custom demands."

"That won't be…"

"My Master graciously accepts your offer as refusal would be a grave insult to you and the great warriors of your clan," Anne hurriedly intervenes, dancing around my faux pas elegantly.

"Yep. What she said." Actor, I am not.

> *I sound nothing like a great warrior and every bit like a giant dork.*

After our initial tussle, Zanatos invites the two of us to dine with him, which is a little strange to say the least. On the surface he is identical to the Kréken that only last week tried to choke the life out of me.

There are some minor differences. His bodysuit is not quite as complete as his predecessor's, and the symbol on his forehead looks like a crucifix with a circle on top of it, rather than a lightning bolt. But at their core they are still essentially one and the same. And the same as the Kréken I saw in the cryo-tube.

This is another perfect clone. What is its number, I wonder?

I can't help but marvel that through the simple act of being able to communicate with each other, we have now gone from deadly enemies to dinner companions.

As I follow him down the narrow tunnels that lead from the ice into his den, I can't help but wish we had the translator with us the last time we were here. Then maybe Anne would not have been forced to break the previous clone's neck.

Probably best not to mention that to him.

Does he know he is a clone? We've established that he can tell he is a prisoner, but how much beyond that can he perceive. And how do I ask that question: "Thanks for dinner, did you know you were a clone?"

It won't help knowing.

Given time, he may have found the etchings on his predecessor's wall and began to question it himself, but instead he has found us.

Exiting into the large underground chamber that comprises his home we share a meal of raw fish, which I stomach by reminding myself it's basically sushi. Zanatos regales us with tales from his life back on Krés and everything he says sounds truly incredible. Outwardly I smile as I listen to him speak about his egg-mates and all the glorious deeds he and his clan have accomplished, but inside I'm filled with a deep sadness.

Ignorance is bliss.

These memories are not really his own. The real Zanatos is back in cryogenics a dozen or so pods away from my own perfectly preserved duplicate.

He doesn't know after all.

I briefly consider telling him the truth, but hearing the pride in his voice I decide I haven't got it in me to break this poor creature's hearts – yes, hearts because apparently he has two of them – the way my own was broken.

Would Zanatos try and kill himself too? Probably not. Suicide is a special human thing, apparently.

When he asks to hear more about my story, Anne proceeds to tell him the legend of Adam X. I try not to blush as I listen to her give him an accurate, albeit exaggerated version of events. Absently rubbing my X when required to hide my surprised expression.

By the time she's done talking, Zanatos has no doubt that I can lead him to freedom. He tells me of the feasts that will be held in my honour when we finally escape the Preservers. Listening to him talk of the future, it makes me think of a life outside captivity.

What are my plans after all this?

Before my trip to the spaceship's core, everything was so clear. I wanted to get off this crazy vessel and get back to – what I thought was – my old life. But what do I want now? Do I want to start a new life? Or just steal Adam Furst's? The right thing to do would be to free him so he can go home – it's what I would do if I was me. But at this point I'm not even sure I can save myself… let alone my other self.

And future selves.

And what about the Preservers? Do I want to stop them? Hurt them? Get some revenge? Or just jump in a drop pod and get the hell away from them?

I ponder the idea for all of a few seconds – that's all it takes – and I know the answer. I just want to get away from this ship!

The rest I'll have to work out later.

X

By my count, it has been almost eight days since our journey began, so it's somewhat frustrating to be back in the Earth habitat. Especially given what had happened in the interim.

> *Was I happier before I started this insane journey?*

I soak up the familiar sights, sounds and smells of the lagoon fondly. After a completely mind-numbingly uneventful ten-hour holdover on Rigilius hanging out with blind cows, it's great to be in a lush landscape.

I am surprised by how much I've missed it. Some boar would be nice! When we come across the waterfall concealing our cave it suddenly occurs to me that this place is as close to a real home as I've ever actually had. Unless you count a tube.

> *Maybe I should just stay here. Living here with Anne wouldn't be the worst thing in the world, would it?*

The moment of weakness passes quickly. Living under the Preservers watchful gaze is not a life worth living. This place is a cage.

A pretty cage, though. And I could share it with a pretty android.

No! No way! I refuse to become just another animal in an alien menagerie. This is not where I'm going to live out the rest of my days.

"So this is what your home world looks like?" Zanatos says, taking in his new surroundings cautiously. "Is it always this warm?"

"This is actually cold by Earth's standards," I point out. I look at his suit and, remembering those uncomfortable days, add, "are you gonna be ok?"

"There is plenty of water here. As long as I keep my gills damp I should be fine," he assures me.

That should rule out a Kréken invasion of Earth any time soon, at least.

"Glad to hear it. Do you need to rest? We have a cave behind that waterfall over there," I inform him.

"Actually, I was hoping you and I could go hunting," he replies with an expectant, predatory grin. "Perhaps we can find one of those carnivorous velociraptors your mate mentioned earlier."

"Maybe later. I'm kinda beat," I yawn. "Oh and she's not my mate. We're just... friends."

"My apologies, friend Adam. I just assumed by the way she speaks of you that the two of you were bonded," he explains as he considers Anne for a moment. "Is she unattractive by human standards?"

I look over at Anne who is thankfully out of earshot – at least human earshot – before whispering back. "No. It's not that. She's *very* attractive. It's just that she's actually an android."

"Android?" he repeats, looking puzzled. "I am unfamiliar with this word."

"An android. Like a robot. A machine built to look like a person. She's not alive."

"Oh," he says quietly, eyes fixed on her back as recognition draws its lines across his alien features. "I have never seen a machine such as this, but I have heard stories."

Good or bad I wonder?

In light of this new information, Zanatos takes a moment to appraise Anne, who stands by the riverbank now only metres away. Suddenly something in his demeanour changes. Like a switch being flipped in his head. His tentacles go taut and he bares his teeth in an angry snarl. Without warning he snatches the pistol from my belt and fires at her repeatedly.

I guess the stories were bad!

"ANNE!" I scream, but it's too late. Three green bolts hit their mark before I'm able to wrestle the gun from his vice-like grip.

"You son of a…" I begin to curse, jamming the weapon up under his chin and itching to pull the trigger.

"The body! Look at the body!" he pleads.

Keeping the pistol firmly wedged under his jaw, I glance over at Anne, who now lays face down, and half submerged in the shallows. That's when I see it – the thing that has Zanatos so rattled.

On Anne's back, floating just above the waterline, something pulsates beneath the material of her bodysuit. Little ripples arc out across the water and the effect is completely unnerving. In fact, it's enough to make me feel sick.

From the top of her spine the source of the movement makes its way out through her left sleeve, emerging onto dry land as a small opaque blob.

"What is that thing?" I ask, bewildered. The pistol falls away from Zanatos' chin as I stare in disbelief.

"It's a parasite! Shoot it! Shoot it now!" he begs. And something in the desperation of his voice cuts through the shock.

Anything that can terrify this big, scary alien must be bad news.

I decide to take him at his word, shooting at the shapeless white mass. Unfortunately the target is small and my first shot goes wide. Realising it's in danger the creature quickly elongates like a snake and slinks into the jungle, my second and third shots hitting nothing but dirt as the parasite disappears into the undergrowth with unnatural speed.

"Blast!" Zanatos curses.

Some legend I turned out to be.

"Can you please explain what the hell is going on?" I ask, rushing over to Anne, who lies wet and motionless. No doubt she's taking a second to compute the tingling sensation in her back.

Does she even feel pain?

"That was The Hunger!" he says, howling in dismay. Then, realising I have no idea what he's talking about adds, "the most dangerous lifeform in the galaxy!"

"That little thing?" I snort in disbelief.

"It does not stay little," he continues. "The Hunger devours organic matter, increasing in size as it does so. Left unchecked it can grow large enough to feed on entire worlds leaving them completely devoid of life."

"Ok. That's bad," I admit. "But what's it doing here? Where did it come from?"

"The empty habitat," Anne provides the answer, rising from the water seemingly unharmed. Zanatos steps back at the sight of her feminine form seemingly rising from the grave. Surely he has never seen a creature take three bullets and enjoy such a quick recovery.

"Androids are tough," I say in way of explanation, then turn back towards the more important matter. "But why was its home planet just an empty void?"

"It would have been kept that way intentionally," Anne speculates, "to keep The Hunger safely contained and unable to feed. The Preservers must have left that detail off their records, perhaps to hide its existence. I was unaware."

Ok, that makes sense.

"Wait a second! If that thing was with us inside the empty habitat, why didn't it try to chow down on me then?" I ask her in disbelief.

Not that I'm complaining. It's about time something on this ship didn't try and eat me.

"You were too big, friend Adam," Zanatos chimes in as he steps behind Anne warily, looking for wounds no doubt. "At this stage the parasite is still small and will only attack prey of equal or lesser size."

"He is correct, Master," she confirms. "Though my databank says The Hunger is a highly intelligent macroscopic virus, not a parasite."

"We're lucky you were here, Zee," I say, truly grateful. "Otherwise we might have accidentally helped that little bugger off the ship."

"It was fortunate you made me curious about your companion's inner workings. If I had not decided to switch my vision to X-ray I would not have noticed its presence," he replies.

"May I ask a favour, Zanatos?" Anne requests, waiting for the big Kréken to nod his consent before she continues. "Your visual acuity is clearly superior to my own. Would you keep watch tonight to make sure The Hunger does not double back and attempt to follow us to the next habitat?"

"It would be my pleasure," he beams, bowing theatrically. "Anything for my new friends."

> *Now we just have to hope that thing doesn't get big enough to eat us all before can get out of here.*

I sit alone by the fire, staring up at the false moon, when I first hear Anne's graceful footfalls approaching. Without a word she takes a seat by my side and we gaze at the stars together, enjoying a moment of comfortable silence.

"It is all a holographic projection," she says after a time, her eyes still locked on the night sky above.

"I figured it was something like that," I reply.

"I heard you talking to Zanatos earlier," she teases.

"About what," I ask with feigned innocence, nerves suddenly a jangle.

I turn to face her. She looks utterly breathtaking bathed in the faux moonlight. Her ethereal beauty stripped straight from the pages of Greek mythology.

"You said you found me, I believe your exact words were, 'very attractive,'" she reminds, turning to meet my gaze.

"You know I do," I admit, feeling the heat rush into my cheeks. "But what does it matter. We're too different."

A man can't be in love with a machine.

"Are we really? Were we not both created by the Preservers?" she points out.

I wince in reply.

"In eight lifetimes I have seen every facet of your character, Adam. Good and bad. Is there anyone in this galaxy who could know you like I do? Anyone who could be more loyal or accepting?"

Her words leave me speechless. I'm lost in her deep blue eyes, not sure how to respond.

Did previous Adams go there? If they didn't know she was an android I can't imagine why they wouldn't. Do I dare ask?

The question just hangs on my lower lip, unsaid.

"According to my databank," she continues, "love is defined as a strong feeling of affection. To take great interest or pleasure in something. Or to feel deep affection or sexual attraction to someone. I am fairly certain this definition accurately describes our relationship. Why do you insist on denying it?"

She's not wrong.

What am I afraid of? The judgment of people I never really met and that I'll probably never meet. With all that has happened, is happening, surely I deserve to feel good, if only for a few moments.

I lean in to kiss her. Gently at first, our lips just touching, then with increased passion as she presses her body into mine. Anne keeps pressing forward and the next thing I know I've fallen back and she is straddling me. The blood rush is epic.

Oh God, I've really wanted this!

I can feel my yearning for her growing and warmth flooding through my body. I'm about to give in and... that's when Zanatos dances by wearing a pink tutu. Wait, what?

Aw crap! I'm dreaming.

I wake up on my old pile of straw and am relieved to find the cave is empty. Throwing my jeans on to hide my shame, I can't help but ponder the meaning behind the embarrassing dream.

It probably just means I'm sexually frustrated. After all I haven't been with a woman in...

I pause remembering that my memories are not actually my own. The reality of the situation dawns like a thump to the back of the head.

I'm a virgin.

And I'm probably in love with a machine. Great. Just great. I'm not even sure it would count if I did go there.

Shaking my head at the thought I throw on my shirt and leave the cave. The sound of raging water soon gives way to the constant din of animal calls that emanate from the jungle around our camp. Dawn light is just starting to peek over the horizon, washing away the gloom, as I begin to search for my friends.

Yet another beautiful day in paradise.

I soon find the two of them a short stroll down the river. Both stand still as statues; Anne on the shore with a dead catfish dangling from one hand, and my alien devotee waist-deep in the lagoon. I wonder what they're doing until, with lightning fast reflexes, Zanatos shoves his hand into the water and plucks out a wriggling trout.

"Are you hungry, friend Adam?" he asks me, throwing his prize to Anne, who catches the slippery sucker with unnatural ease.

"Yeah, I am actually," I reply. "But I'll have mine cooked this time if that's alright."

"Cooked?" the big alien repeats, as he wades back to shore. "What is this word, cooked?"

"It is a style of food preparation customary on Earth that involves heating the ingredients of a meal before their consumption," Anne explains.

"You gotta try it," I encourage with a big smile.

Zanatos' expression is review enough. He looks about as impressed with eating my meal cooked as I was eating his raw, but to his credit he finishes his meal without complaint. As he backs away from the flames of the fire I realise how off-putting the heat must be to a Kréken. Especially in that suit.

Fire is not his friend.

When our bellies are full and Anne's pulse emitter is fully charged, we prepare for the next leg of our journey. Zanatos does one last infrared scan of our surroundings as I grab my coat.

"The next habitat is a representation of the Kaa'lik home world," Anne informs us. "It will be an extremely hazardous journey. I recommend caution."

"Kaa'lik," Zanatos announces, kicking at the dirt. His tentacles twitch. "We have a problem, friend Adam."

"Is it The Hunger? Has it come back?" I ask glancing about nervously.

"No. There has been no sign of the parasite since yesterday," he assures me.

"Macroscopic virus," Anne interjects annoyingly.

"It is the Kaa'lik home world that concerns me," Zanatos continues. "I know this planet: it is an inferno. My kind do not survive long in such conditions."

"He is correct Master," Anne agrees reluctantly. "It is unlikely Zanatos will survive the ten hour wait: I recommend he stays behind. We can open a portal for him from the outer ring."

"Isn't that too dangerous?" I remind her. "Didn't you say that exposing lifeforms to that much pressure can make their head explode?"

"I do not wish my head exploded," Zanatos points out, rather needlessly.

"It will not be pleasant," Anne confirms. "But Krékens are considerably more resilient than humans. I am confident he will survive the process."

"Then it is decided," Zanatos asserts.

"I don't know about this," I throw out there. "I'm not that comfortable about leaving you here. Not with that blob thing still around."

"The Hunger is not what concerns me," Zanatos says, waving away my objections. "It will be some time before it is large enough to threaten me and I can see it coming from quite a distance. It is breaking my oath to you that bothers me more."

"What? That life debt thing? As far as I'm concerned you repaid that when you warned us about the slimy hitchhiker hiding inside Anne."

"That is kind of you to say, but I am afraid it doesn't matter, the android is correct. As shameful as it is to admit, the smartest course of action is for me to remain behind while you two go on ahead. I will hold you back on Kaa'lik."

"Take this," Anne says, handing him her pistol. "It will help you repel The Hunger until we return."

"Thank you," he replies, accepting the gift. "Now go, the both of you. And take care, friend Adam. We are kin now. I look forward to feasting with you once we have escaped this accursed vessel."

"Me too, Zee. We'll send for you soon. You have my word," I promise him.

Wow, I'm actually going to miss his ugly mug.

Anne opens the portal and disappears through it, but I hesitate for a moment. Standing on the threshold, I glance over my shoulder, give him one last reassuring wave then step into the light hoping I'm able to keep that promise.

XI

"Are you ok Adam?" Anne asks as I stumble into Kaa'lik, but I can barely suck in the breath required to answer. The moment I emerge through the doorway my senses are assaulted so hard by the stifling heat and foul stench of sulphur I'm almost knocked right off my feet.

Yuck! Smells like rotten eggs.

As my eyes adjust to the dim light I begin to squint through the smoke, scanning the volcanic craters that belch putrid ash into the atmosphere. High above a thick blanket of black clouds choke out the sky and prevent any genuine sunlight from reaching the surface. In fact the only illumination is provided by the pools of molten hot lava that dot the landscape. Everything touched by the light takes on a demonic, red glow.

"Wow," I attempt, but can barely get a word out without coughing. "Zee wasn't kidding when he said this place was an inferno. It's hotter than hell in here."

Still active, the universal translator starts to echo my sentiments in Kréken until I shut it down with a quick double tap and the word, "end."

I then strip off my jacket as fast as I can to make the muggy temperature a fraction more tolerable. Tying it around my waist, I glance at Anne who is completely unperturbed by the temperature change.

Of course.

"Take this, Master," Anne says, pulling a red power pack from her belt and handing it to me.

"Zanatos isn't here anymore, so you can quit calling me *Master*," I tell her, taking the new clip in my sweaty hands, then almost dropping it. "What's with this? My pistol still has a three-quarter charge."

"Loading that will allow you to fire lethal shots," she explains. "You will need more than stun bolts if we encounter a Kaa'lik drone."

"You're not worried I'll try to blow my brains out again?" I ask her, ejecting the old power pack and shoving it in my pocket.

"Observing the previous clones I have noticed you have a tendency to prioritise the needs of others over your own. Now that Zanatos is relying on you to secure his freedom, I have calculated a ninety-percent chance that you will not harm yourself."

Plus, I could just jump into a lava pit if I was really determined to end it.

I lean over a precipice and recoil at the searing heat like an elephant who has seen a mouse. She's right though. I'm as determined to help Zanatos escape as I am myself. I admit this revelation in a moment of introspection that ends with a sigh. That's the whole reason I wanted to be a police officer.

To protect and serve.

I realise then that eight lifetimes living with my various clones means she probably knows me better than I do. But one thing she failed to mention was that I'm just as concerned about disappointing her as I am Zanatos. The insight reminds me of the dream I had the night before.

Does it really mean what I think it does?

"Adam, we've been spotted. My auditory sensors are detecting something approaching our position," she warns me. "And fast!"

Happy for an excuse to stop interrogating myself, I concentrate instead on finding the source of what Anne is picking up. At first the only thing I can make out is the steady sound of bubbling lava, but eventually I hear it too. A faint buzzing noise growing louder by the second.

"What is that?" I frown. Both our gazes slowly lift from the molten pools and lock on the smoky clouds above. "I think… is it…"

"It's coming from the clouds, in all likelihood the drone I spoke of a moment ago. I recommend caution," she advises, aiming her left palm at the sky in readiness.

"Can we reason with it?" I ask, fumbling to insert the new power pack into my weapon, but my hands are swollen from the heat and sweaty to boot.

"No," comes Anne's disappointing reply. "Without a queen to issue instructions the drone will be a mindless beast intent on killing you. Our only option is to use lethal force."

I look at the clip still clasped uselessly in my hand in sudden panic.

Crap.

I fumble to get my gun loaded and point it up just in time to see what looks like an enormous praying mantis burst through the clouds.

Anne begins firing almost immediately and I follow suit a fraction of a second later. The drone is lightning fast and for a time it evades everything we throw at it, but eventually our persistence pays off. A few of my shots punch through its massive wings, turning them to Swiss cheese and forcing it into a freefall.

Glancing at Anne triumphantly, I fail to notice the danger is not yet over. The drone is resourceful, using what's left of its wings to turn a straight drop into a barely controlled glide, closing the distance between us at some speed.

"Look out," Anne warns, pushing me aside just in the nick of time. As I tumble to safety across the ash and sharp rocks, the giant insect lands on top of her, mandibles clicking furiously. Before she can resume firing, the beast runs one of its stabbing appendages through her back.

It pins her down, making it impossible for her to fire off a clean shot.

"ANNE!" I scream, causing the insect to swivel its head in my direction. I'm already jumping to my feet. I fire repeatedly at the creature's head, a volley of lasers cutting the air.

One of my shots meets its mark and the Kaa'lik's bulbous, yellow eye explodes into a shower of gore and ichor. Screeching in agony, the wounded beast flings Anne's impaled body through the air and into a nearby lava pit. As I watch her sink into the molten liquid I lose all semblance of control.

She's gone!

"NOOOOO!" I bellow in rage.

I continue to fire as I run towards the towering threat. My shots pepper through the thrashing insect's exoskeleton, and I watch the beast fall apart with perverse satisfaction. Antennae, mandible, thorax – all are shredded by my endless onslaught until there is nothing left of the Kaa'lik drone. Just an oozing, mutilated mess.

As the desire for revenge floods from my body I begin to tremble. I run to the edge of the volcanic crater to check on Anne. I can barely stand the heat as I peer into the pool of molten rock searching for any signs of movement. Desperation hammers my heart.

Nothing could survive that.

The adrenaline that fuelled me only moments ago fades into sorrow. I fall to my knees and stare at the harsh, darkened ground, my feelings for Anne now painfully clear.

Anne's gone.

If I had really believed she was just a machine losing her wouldn't hurt like this. I loved her and I didn't have the guts to admit it, not even to myself.

"Why didn't I tell you?" I say aloud, my voice sounding hollow in my ears. Too exhausted to even cry.

"What did you wish to tell me, Adam?" a familiar voice inquires, yanking me violently from my grief.

I see her then, rising like a phoenix from the flames. Her synthetic flesh burnt away by the red hot liquid, revealing her crystal endoskeleton in all its glory. She looks like something from a horror movie – a glittering, skeletal form wading through the magma.

Anyone else would run screaming in the opposite direction, but all I can think about is how much I want to embrace her.

"Anne! You're alive! I can't believe it!" I cry out, my voice raspy and a wide grin plastered across my face.

"Why can you not believe it?" Anne asks in a tone so straight it might as well be the horizon. "I'm standing in front of you."

I nod stupidly, "yes you are."

"The majority of my body is comprised of lonsdaleite," she points out, "and can withstand temperatures in excess of two thousand degrees Celsius."

"That's not what I meant," I begin to explain, moving in to hug her.

"I would advise against that," she warns, stopping me in my tracks with my arms outstretched. "While your show of affection is appreciated, touching me right now would almost certainly result in serious burns to your arms, cheek and upper torso."

"Right. Of course," I grin sheepishly.

"Now I believe there was something you wanted to tell me?" she asks again.

"Oh that," I hesitate.

I'm not ready for this.

"Uh... I just wanted to tell you..." I can almost hear my brain ticking over. "Um... I think you're amazing."

This is not the right time to pour my heart out to her, I realise. I'll tell her when she isn't half melted and surrounded by bubbling sulphur and insect gizzard.

"Thank you, Adam," Anne responds, looking down at the remains of the drone that attacked us. "You're amazing, too."

I have my moments.

"This landscape is full of caves," Anne says straight back to business. "I suggest we find one. It is going to take me a while to recharge."

And so we sit in a Kaa'lik sauna for what seems like an eternity, silent and sweaty. A man with an X on his forehead and his crystalline protector.

XII

After departing the Kaa'lik habitat I welcome the
fat raindrops that strike my face like a desert toad
– tongue out and fervently. They fall from above,
washing away all traces of the previous volcanic
hellhole from my body. I open my mouth and let the
cool drops soothe my raw throat. As the moment
passes, I'm left feeling refreshed and renewed.

As Anne closes the portal and steps to my side, the
rain begins to bead on her exposed skeleton until she
is sparkling like an angel.

This must be heaven.

"This is Flora One," Anne states, ruining the illusion.

It's well named. That becomes abundantly clear
once I realise the spongy ground beneath my feet is
actually a gigantic sunflower, or at least a species with
similarities. Carefully, I make my way over to the edge
of one of the giant petals to take a better look at this
strange new world. Mammoth blossoms stretch off in
every direction, filling the air with a heavenly aroma.

*This is what the world must look like to an ant
back on Earth.*

The thought makes me feel small and insignificant. "What's gonna try to kill us this time?" I ask, once I've had my fill of the beautiful sights and smells. "Killer flowers? Giant bees? Hay fever?"

"None of those are present as far as I am aware," she replies. "But there are other dangerous predators here. I recommend caution."

"You always recommend caution," I tease.

"And I am always right to do so," she retorts.

Remembering the last encounter, I check how much ammo I have left.

Still got half a charge.

"Hey, there's plenty of water here," I point out, putting my hand into the light breeze and watching rain splash upon my palm. "Maybe we should bring Zanatos through now?"

"That would mean spending an additional ten hours in a dangerous and hostile environment," she begins to explain. "And then we would be forced to leave him behind yet again as the next habitat is a desert world he would find extremely unpleasant."

Not again. I just got away from the heat.

I imagine the amphibious Kréken trying to survive in a sandy wasteland and acknowledge her point with a begrudging nod.

"I believe the most prudent course of action would be to follow our original plan," she concludes.

As if on command, an enormous shadow momentarily blots out what sun is splicing through the clouds. Glancing up I see something that looks disturbingly like a dragon glide overhead in the far distance. It's big, whatever it is.

Here we go again.

Thankfully it does not appear to notice the two little specks down below and continues on its course. "So, what the hell is it this time?" I ask nervously.

"A Floran fire lizard," she states offhandedly, scanning the breadth of our flower perch. "We are too exposed up here. We should head down beneath the canopy where we can better conceal ourselves."

"We must be like a hundred feet up," I point out, finger stretched out towards the tree trunks disappearing off beneath the flower as evidence. "How are we supposed to get down?"

"We climb of course," she replies, using her laser to shear through one of the petals where it connects at the base.

With no skin to hide her inner workings, I can see the inside of Anne's arm glowing red hot as she uses her laser cannon. I watch with fascination until the cut is complete and the large petal floats gently down into the dark below.

Through the newly made gap I can see the green stem and the considerable distance between us and the ground. One hundred feet was an understatement. My gut clenches in protest at the thought of having to climb down from such a height.

"I don't think I can do this," I tell her.

"You can ride down on my back," she offers.

Why not, it's not like I have any masculinity left at this point.

Swallowing my pride, again, I put my arms around her cold, crystalline neck and hop onto her back. The heat from her laser arm is at odds with the cool of her shoulders, and the smooth surface is challenging to get a grip on. I end up latching my legs around her like a Koala might hug a gum tree. Squeezing my eyes shut, I don't open them again until I'm certain Anne has piggybacked me all the way down.

I untie my legs and jump to the ground, trying to stand tall and strong like I didn't just get carried to safety... again. "Thanks for that," I manage.

But Anne is already exploring our surroundings. We find ourselves fenced by a forest of flower stems as thick as trees. We search vainly for a place to hole up, but inviting little nooks and crannies only welcome us to puddles and mud. The light does not help: what filters down is weak at best and heavily coloured by the petals above.

It's kinda like disco lighting.

With nowhere suitable presenting itself, we decide to make our own shelter in a small clearing using the giant yellow petal Anne cut down moments before. Together we flip it over, bend it and use sharp sticks as pegs.

With the sides pinned in place, the end result is a rather impressive looking tent, big enough for two full sized adults to crawl into. Once I've taken a few moments to admire our handy work I pile some fern leaves in as a makeshift bed. I then climb inside with a sigh, looking forward to spending some precious moments horizontal.

I move to one side and smooth out the ferns for Anne, then look at her expectantly.

"I'll stand watch," she replies.

My dreams are full of untold horrors, but they don't last long before they're distorted by a dark figure looming over me. I almost jump out of my skin as the reverie breaks into reality, heart pounding in panic. For a second I fear the Preservers have come for me, but as my eyes adjust I recognise Anne's translucent skull-like visage.

"Jesus! You scared the hell out of me. What's going on?" I rub at my eyes only to see Kaa'lik ash come away on my fists.

I guess the rain didn't wash away all the grime after all.

"I apologise for waking you, but my auditory sensors have detected something nearby," she tells me quietly.

"Aw crap," I curse, scrambling out of the tent.

"I do not believe it to be a threat," she clarifies.

"Oh. Well that's a first," I reply, re-holstering my half-drawn weapon. "So what do you think it is?"

"I cannot be certain, but it sounds like someone crying," Anne replies confused.

I hear it then – beneath the faint pitter-patter of raindrops hitting the floral canopy way above – a barely audible sobbing. I attempt to hone in on the sound, following it deeper into the dim forest with Anne trailing just a few steps behind.

Could it be an alien trap? With my luck anything's possible.

As we go deeper into the undergrowth, the dark begins to hug in close. A curious light shines from inside Anne's head, providing dim illumination as we creep towards the sound. Seeing her in this form, sneaking through the bushes, is disturbing at best.

Eventually I give in to my curiosity: "what's with the light?" I whisper.

"I do not understand your question. You will need to be more specific," she replies.

"The light," I add, tapping the X on my forehead for added emphasis. "Why is there a light coming out of your head?"

"The light you are referring to is emanating from the nuclear battery located inside my skull," she replies in that wonderfully unemotional tone.

"Nuclear!" I cough, forgetting my volume for a moment and turning to face her. We freeze as the crying stops for one second. Two seconds. Three seconds. Then it starts again.

"Is that thing safe?" I whisper, staring aghast.

"It is. As I have stated previously, I would never inflict harm or, by my own inaction, allow harm to befall you."

"Not on purpose you wouldn't. But what if that thing gets damaged or something, could you explode?"

"Theoretically, if I were to lower my radiation shielding and open my access port," she points out, indicating the circular mark on her brow. "Then remove the battery and make some minor modifications, I could create a demon core."

"A demon core?" I repeat confused.

"A small nuclear bomb, like the ones used on Earth," she explains. "But my primary function is to ensure your survival, so I would never allow such a thing to happen – well at least not in your vicinity."

For a moment I consider what having access to a nuke could mean, but dismiss the thought quickly. It would be pretty satisfying blowing those Preserver bastards to kingdom come, but I could never go through with it.

What about Zanatos?

Even assuming Anne and I could escape the blast, I wouldn't risk hurting all the other innocent lifeforms aboard this ship. Letting the thought slide, I begin picking my way through the foliage again.

It's not long before we have tracked the sobbing to a small huddled figure. It's curled up in the shadow of a giant flower stem, much like a fallen seed. I keep my distance at first, not wanting to distress the poor creature any more than it already is.

"Hello there," I say in my most soothing voice.

The stranger jumps to their feet, clearly startled. Shrouded in the darkness, I'm just able to make out a thick head of curly hair and a distinctly female shape. She stares at me.

This is no threat. This is just a scared little girl.

"Adam you…"

"I got this one," I cut Anne off. I've been trained in this sort of thing. I just need to set her at ease. I put my hands up in the air and take a step closer. "We're not here to hurt you, we heard you crying."

Silence greets the statement. I try again, "are you ok?"

More silence. I look back at Anne and shrug, then notice her patiently tapping her wrist.

"Adam you may want to set the universal translator to Floran," she suggests, without a hint of sarcasm.

"Oh." I silently curse my own stupidity before doing exactly as she instructed. Once the UT has been activated, I try again.

"Don't be afraid. My name is Adam and this is Anne. What's your name?" I ask.

No answer again, but the small silhouette seems slightly less skittish now that I'm speaking her native tongue. She continues to give me the silent treatment though, just like Anne did the first time I met her.

It's enough to give a guy a complex.

"Hey. You don't think she's an android do you?" I whisper over my shoulder.

"No. She is most definitely organic. My auditory sensors are detecting an increase in her respiration and heartbeat," she assures me.

"It's ok if you don't want to talk," I continue, turning my attention back to the mystery women. "But I think you'd be a lot safer with us than out here alone. At the very least we can show you a better place to hide. What do you say?"

She seems to think it over a moment and, after a quick glance back to her previous and completely unsatisfactory hidey hole, cautiously moves towards us. After almost a month of close encounters both strange and wondrous, I didn't think there was anything that could step out of those shadows that could shock me, but I was dead wrong.

The first surprise comes when I see her face. Not because it is alien, but because it looks so completely human. The girl looks young. Sixteen, maybe seventeen. Her dirty face is streaked by tears, revealing the pale, lightly freckled cheeks beneath. Green eyes wide as saucers and still puffy from crying peer out with suspicion. Her mud-spattered forehead is marked with what looks like the number eight. A mane of strawberry blonde ringlets frame her face and hang down to her small perky breasts, bringing me to the second surprise.

When she has stepped fully into the light, I realise a thick layer of mud is the only thing keeping her from being completely naked.

"Oh I'm so sorry," I apologise, averting my gaze.

Keeping my eyes pointed upwards I untie the jacket from my waist and feebly attempt to brush off the ash.

I hand it to her so she can cover herself. Once she has slipped on my coat and zipped it up, I peek again with one eye and am relieved to see the jacket is long enough on her to behave as a dress.

"That's better. Our camp is not too far from here. It's more of the same really, but not quite as dark and there's a tent that will keep you dry," I assure her.

She responds with silence, instead just watching me closely, so I let it hang there a moment before adding, "right then. Follow me."

XXXX

Back at camp our new guest heads straight into the tent – where she can stay hidden – while Anne and I remain outside to discuss what we're going to do with her. I flick off the universal translator and look to Anne for guidance.

"She is clearly traumatised," Anne points out.

"Not surprising," I can't help but agree. "If I didn't have you to dress and feed me I probably would've ended up exactly the same."

"Incorrect. You would have ended up dead," she reminds me. Harsh, but I know she wasn't trying to hurt my feelings.

Thinking about what happened to the first and second Adam clones fills me with shame, but also untold respect for our new friend. She was alone and surrounded by monsters just like my duplicates. But despite the odds being stacked firmly against her, she didn't give up.

And she did it in the nude.

"It's kinda freaky how human she looks," I point out, changing the subject.

"The resemblance is not coincidental," Anne begins to explain. "The Floran race was created when Paracas slavers began abducting humans around four thousand BC by your Earth calendar. The slaves were put to work on Flora One and after a little DNA resequencing became a completely separate species to your own."

Abducted by the Paracas and then by the Preservers! And I thought my luck was bad.

I grimace at the thought. It's not fair. None of this is fair. "What is so important on this planet that these aliens needed to abduct innocent people and force them to work on another world?"

"Pollen found on Flora One is used to make a variety of illicit drugs sold all over the galaxy," Anne reveals. "Unfortunately the pollen is too delicate to be picked by artificial means, hence the use of organics with thumbs and numerous deft digits."

"Slavers and drug dealers," I snarl, furrowing my brow in anger. "These Paracas creatures sound like some truly evil bastards."

"Good or evil is subjective," she replies, sounding every bit the android. "According to my databank, your people have enslaved one another and partaken in recreational drug use all throughout human history. By your definition that would make your species equally as evil?"

Yeah, but I never did any of that.

"Point taken," I concede. "Still, I feel bad for her if she has memories of being a slave. Even if they are fake."

"It is an inefficient use of your time feeling bad about something you cannot change, Adam," she chides.

"You're right. I can't change her past, but I can change her future," I say determinedly. "We have to help her."

"By help her I take it you mean liberate her from this vessel," Anne clarifies. "I would be remiss not to point out that every additional person you try to rescue from the Preservers decreases your own chances of successfully escaping."

"Noted. But we're doing it anyway, 'cos it's the right thing to do," I say with finality.

"Right and wrong are also subjective opinions. Perhaps you should ask her what she wants?" Anne suggests, refusing to let the matter drop.

As if she'd want to stay here.

"Fine. I'll ask." I concede, humouring her even though I'm already certain of the answer. Assured, I take a few cautious steps towards the tent, flick on the translator, and then duck down to view its sole occupant.

"Hi... err..." I begin to greet her, then realise I don't know the girl's name. I turn back towards Anne and whisper: "I still don't know what to call her. It's too bad we don't have that chalk any more."

"Guano," she says.

"What?" I frown, not sure what she means.

"That was not chalk you found in our cave. It was petrified bat faeces, more commonly referred to as guano," she explains.

Ew! Gross!

I smell my fingers and I'm hit with a nose-full of sulphur for my troubles. "Why didn't you say something?" I wrinkle my brow in disgust, recalling how I twirled it between my thumb and forefinger.

And for hours.

"As I mentioned to you earlier, my secondary function required me to remain silent," Anne points out again. "So there is no reason for you to be embarrassed by your actions."

"Easy for you to say, you weren't the one playing with bat shit!" I compose myself and look back towards our guest. I go to double tap the UT, only to realise it is already on.

Dammit!

I catch a hint of amusement cross the girl's face. Just a flash, but I let her have it. I'd laugh at me, too.

"Ah, hey in there. Could you come out for a second? I need to ask you something."

She pops her head through the opening. Her eyes dart anxiously in all directions searching for potential threats. The jerky movement of her head makes her red hair sway, briefly exposing ears that end in sharp points at the top.

Not completely human looking after all.

I offer her a reassuring hand, hoping she'll take it despite what she heard about my guano adventures.

"It's ok. There's nothing to be afraid of."

She takes my hand in hers and that's when we hear a deafening crash. All our eyes widen as they turn towards the disturbance. Huge stems appear to be parting as something big brushes them aside with frightening strength. The ground trembles with each step as the unknown threat makes its way closer and closer. The girl's grip on my hand tightens ten-fold.

Has she seen whatever this is before?

I turn to Anne for some sage like advice. "I believe you are mistaken, Adam. It appears there is something of which to be afraid."

XIII

Anne takes the lead as we make our getaway and I drag the Floran girl in my wake. The three of us run for our lives, dodging and weaving through the undergrowth. From behind, the mysterious behemoth can be heard roaring in frustration as it attempts to navigate its massive bulk between the thick flower stems that stand between it and us – its next meal.

Why does everything want to eat me?!

"How long 'til we can open the next portal?" I shout between ragged breathes.

"Two minutes and sixteen seconds," Anne replies, unnaturally calm given the circumstance. "Longer if I am forced to fire on our pursuer."

"Could you kill it if you did?!" I wonder, but I already know the answer.

"Before it kills you and the Floran girl?" she asks rhetorically. "Unlikely."

"Then don't bother," I instruct her, leaping over an exposed root that threatens to trip up the whole escape. "Just get that door open!"

As I silently will Anne's pulse emitter to charge faster, I realise that the rhythmic pounding of the predator's heavy footsteps aren't getting any louder. That means it isn't gaining on us despite its huge strides.

We're losing it! We're gonna make it!

No sooner has the thought crossed my mind, than I feel the girl's grip slip from mine. She tumbles alongside a shriek of pain, the loud sound exploding from her lips as she hits the ground hard. I bite down on my lip to prevent my own yelp in anger in fear of further identifying our direction to whatever beast is hot on our tail.

I had to jinx us.

Instantly those thunderous footsteps are incoming again, each bang bringing death one stride closer. Without any thought for my own wellbeing I turn back and try to lift the girl to her feet. After a few hobbled steps and pained cries I realise she has a twisted ankle and won't be running again any time soon.

In the thirty seconds it takes for all of this to transpire, our pursuer closes the distance. It's then that I get my first good look at it.

A snout full of needle sharp teeth bears down on us. It pokes out from beneath beady orange eyes with dark slitted pupils. Its eyes glow in the darkness as if illuminated from within by some kind of internal flame.

It's a freakin' dragon! The one I saw earlier.

Dread rockets through me as it lunges forward, mouth wide and ready to swallow us whole.

This is it. Eaten.

I squeeze the girl close and bury her face into my chest. I try to stare it down, but at the last second I close my eyes.

Snap!

I'm still here.

Snap!

I pry an eye open just enough to see teeth inches away from my face.

Snap!

The jaws clack together again, releasing the reptile's putrid breath in a cloud right across my face. My hair blows back, instantly drenched by something horrifying.

Saliva?

The beast's wide body had become wedged between two thick stems, I realise. I take advantage of the momentary reprieve and, trembling, scoop the girl up into my arms. As I flee, the fire-breathing mega lizard swings its long, scaly neck from side to side in a desperate attempt to dislodge itself.

Fearful of losing its meal, the dragon goes to plan B. It spits a huge ball of fire at us hoping to cook us as we run. It is only the timely intervention of Anne, who places her near indestructible body between us and the flames, which prevents us from being barbequed alive. The heat coils around her frame and then reaches out at the hairs standing at attention on my arms. But ultimately, it's foiled.

Saved again.

Now in the lead I push forward, my legs burning with every step. Arms in agony as the girl's tiny frame bounces in my grasp. Anne trails a few paces behind, determined to take the next blow. In the distance I hear the sound of the thick stems cracking as the dragon finally frees itself. The footsteps recommence their baseline. Desperate I jump through a wall of thorny weeds and into the clearing beyond… only to find a sheer, stone wall.

A dead end.

I look for some sort of handholds we could use to climb it, but there aren't any. I turn to face my death, clutching the girl close as I pant with exhaustion. The bushes move and I brace myself for the worst.

Oh thank God, it's just Anne.

She steps through the bushes as cool as a cucumber and calmly utters the seven most beautiful words I've ever heard:

"My pulse emitter is now at maximum."

The doorway to salvation opens a few metres ahead and even though I'm completely exhausted and my legs feel like jelly, I summon the last of my energy and power through it to safety.

XXXX

Coming out the other side my momentum carries me forward a few more paces before my legs finally give out. Conscious of the girl in my arms, I twist my body as I fall, so that we land side by side.

The last thing she needs is to be crushed.

Laying there I stare up at the aqua blue sky and take a moment to catch my breath. The girl is grabbing at her head in clear pain and I'm about to ask what is wrong when I realise I never got a chance to tell her what portal travel is like.

You get used to the pain.

Anne emerges from the portal a few seconds later and the flames blowing out against her back suggest it was a close thing.

She steps over to where I lay sprawled out in the soft, warm sand. "Have you sustained damage?" she asks, staring down at me quizzically.

Before I can answer, a sound I had hoped to never hear again takes us all by surprise. The dragon's roar fills the air as its horned head thrusts through the doorway. Before Anne can even turn she is swallowed whole with one mighty chomp. I'm stunned.

Anne?!

I wait for the next bite, resigned to what has appeared to my fate all along. To be eaten alive. But instead, everything goes eerily still.

No sound.

No movement.

The beast just stares at us as if frozen in time. The only sound to be heard is that of my young companion scrambling away from the motionless reptile through the sand. Her ankle dragging uselessly behind her.

"It's ok, I'm pretty sure it's dead," I say to her with listless confidence.

Getting up I cautiously step around the scaly, green skull. My suspicions are confirmed when I see that the dragon's body is nowhere to be seen.

Bad move, big guy.

I wince at the creature's gruesome end. Anne was the only thing keeping the portal open and when it ate her the doorway shut down, cleanly separating its head from its body and cauterising the wound.

Did it have time to swallow? I need to get that mouth open, Anne could still be in there.

I tentatively reach out towards the dragon's mouth, looking into its eyes for any sign of life. When they remain motionless, I shove my fingers inside its tough, unforgiving lips, feeling the heat still lingering in its teeth. I brace a foot between the lizard's huge lips and attempt to pry open its massive jaws.

"Give me a hand!" I call to the Floran girl, who just stares at me like I'm crazy.

Straining, I soon feel the yellow reptilian teeth begin to shudder as they slowly part. Not because of my efforts, but because Anne is using her considerable strength to free herself from within. She soon has the beast's mouth spread wide enough for her to leap out before it can slam shut again.

Saliva drips from her crystalline form, a stark contrast to the beautiful beads of rain she had carried only a few hours earlier. "Always getting eaten," I tease her, trying to hide my happiness to see her alive.

In response, Anne just stares at me blankly. I imagine she would be scowling if her skeletal face was able to portray such emotion.

I miss how she looked before her lava bath.

As I slump down into the sand to gather my breath and let my aching muscles recover, a thought tumbles out: "Anne, can you use our dead friend here to grow back your skin?"

"Yes. This head contains more than enough organic matter for me to fully regenerate my synthetic flesh," she replies.

"He ate you first, right? Seems only fair you eat him back," I add playfully.

"Fair and unfair, like right and wrong, are subjective opinions. Nonetheless ,I can eat the lizard's head in order to regenerate if that is your preference," her robotic visage queries deadpan.

"I'm good either way," I lie. "But our new friend might be more comfortable if you didn't look quite so... scary."

Truth is, she doesn't seem bothered by Anne's appearance in the slightest. And hasn't since the moment we met, I realise. I guess robots must be commonplace back on Flora One.

Caught up in the prospect of getting the old Anne back, I fail to notice the alien girl's deteriorating mental state. She is not taking our recent brush with death as well as we are, veterans that we've become. A tiny sniffle catches my attention and I notice she is once again sobbing.

Have I become an old-hand at death-defying escapes already?

"I'm such an idiot," I chastise myself as I help her up. "You're clearly upset and here I am mucking around."

I hug her reassuringly, gently pressing one of her pointy ears into my chest and gently patting her back until she's all cried out.

"There, there, Spock," I soothe. "It's all gonna be ok. I won't let anything bad happen to you."

"Spock?" Anne repeats. "Curious. I was unaware you had learned the identity of the Floran female."

"I haven't, but we've gotta call her something until she decides to talk to us," I point out.

"True. But why not homo florus specimen eight?" But one look at my expression is enough to quell that notion. "As you wish. The Floran female will now be designated: Spock."

It takes me all of two minutes to learn everything I need to know about our new location. Planet Buudaki, as Anne calls it, is nothing but blazing heat and burning sand. I begin my time there lounging in the shadow of the fallen dragon – the only place in sight safe from the relentless red giant that takes up most of the sky.

I'm getting really sick of hot planets.

With my shirt off and wrapped around my head like a turban, Spock remains by my side. She's soon dozing, her head nestled on my bare, sweaty shoulder. I do my best to shield her bare legs from the intense sun, but there's little I can do.

> *This heat won't be doing the swelling in that ankle any favours, either.*

Meanwhile Anne – who has no reason to fear sunburn or dehydration – spends her time on the opposite side of the decapitated head, consuming the organic matter needed to restore her lost flesh.

I sit in the uncomfortable silence for hours on end, listening to the horror story unfolding behind me. Sweat pools in every crevasse and the salt stings the fresh cuts on my arms. Fresh ones, earned during my latest forest escape.

> *It could have been so much worse.*

My tongue flicks at the crunchy sand granules that have somehow found their way into my parched mouth. At least, until my tongue starts to struggle against the dryness. The sensation is painfully unpleasant, so I turn my attention to Spock's gentle snoring, the only thing to listen to outside Anne's ripping and chewing.

> *I could murder a steak, right now. Oh and a beer. A beer would go down nicely.*

I can feel my lips beginning to crack and the air coming in my mouth becomes so hot it starts to hurt. I'm just starting to wonder whether I could stomach drinking my own urine when I notice the rhythmic sound of Anne eating her meal has stopped.

"Are you ok over there?" I call out.

"Yes. I am now operating at optimal capacity," she replies, stepping back into view looking like her old self, but with one minor difference. Her dark hair is now cropped short. Seeing her restored fills me with joy; the elation as quenching as a cool drink.

Well almost.

I look over her milky white skin and familiar curves. The dragon's skin she has fashioned into a passable top and sarong, too. I take in the way her new hair frames her face and draws attention to her perfect cheek bones.

I want to tell her how much I missed that face. How beautiful she is. That I may be in love with her. That I don't care that she's an android and I'm a human being. And that I want to spend the rest of my life with her. But all that comes out of my mouth is:

"You've changed your hair."

"Not intentionally. My hair does not regenerate as quickly as my synthetic flesh," she explains. "Does my current appearance displease you?"

"No," I blurt out. "Not at all. You look..."

Good? Amazing? Breathtaking?

Before I can choose the least embarrassing superlative I feel Spock lift her head and physically tense. Her fingernails digging into my arm as she gasps in surprise.

What?! What is it now?!

I follow her gaze to Anne and realise that to her, it must look like a complete stranger standing over us. "It's ok Spock," I soothe. "That's Anne."

"I've regenerated," Anne adds, with that calm voice of hers. The words mollify Spock somewhat, but I can still see she is confused by the android's drastic change in appearance. I would be too.

"This is how she looked when I first met her," I try to clarify. "When you first met her she was all damaged 'cos she got thrown into a pit of lava by a giant bug. But now she's fixed. So what to you must seem like a new Anne is actually the old Anne to me."

She's looking at me like I'm a raving lunatic. Maybe I am?

"Hello, Spock," Anne tells her by way of a fresh introduction. "While I underwent repairs, I also took the liberty of creating you some new clothing." Anne holds out a pair of dragon skin garments similar to her own.

The red-headed girl lets the offering hang there, before snatching it from Anne's grasp with a baleful glare. The exchange is weird. Why didn't Spock have a problem with Anne when she was all scary and skeletal? But something about the way she looks now sure seems to bother her.

If she ever starts talking, I'll make that my first question.

"How long until we can jump to the next habitat?" I ask Anne, pretending not to notice the awkward exchange.

"There are no more habitats. Our next stop is the outer ring of this vessel."

And freedom.

Her words fill me with hope. Well kind of. There's also something else I feel. Something I can't quite grasp.

Is that fear?

XIV

With Anne's words ringing in my ears and little else to do, my mind begins to wander. It's been ten long days since I first left the Earth enclosure and during that time I have faced every threat imaginable. Frigid cold, blistering heat, the ocean's depths, and an endless collection of blood thirsty beasts determined to turn me into their next meal. Yet despite all those hardships, I have survived and now stand at the finish line, only one step away from freedom.

When Anne opens the portal, I step into the outer ring and it's almost anti-climactic. No fire-breathing dragons or planet destroying blobs. No army of Preservers with weapons cocked, ready to herd me back to my cage.

Have they even noticed I'm missing yet?

All there is to greet us are the same curved walls I recognise from my time in the inner core. But the outer ring contains no cryogenic tubes; in fact, it contains nothing. No exposed cables running down its length. No windows, computer screens or buttons to break up its smooth surface. I can't even see a seam where one sheet of metal attaches to another. Just cold, grey metal as far as the eye can see.

How boring. These Preservers need a new interior decorator.

A barely audible hum can be heard beneath our footsteps. The plod, plod of my feet echo through the halls, alongside the dragging sound of Spock's ankle as it trails slightly behind her.

Am I actually gonna get off this ship without ever facing my captors?

There's something about that which seems wrong. What they've done to me, to Zanatos, to Spock… even to Anne and her luckless primary objective. I guess I'll just have to settle for flipping them off through the drop pod's window after we launch.

We don't walk for long before Anne stops in front of a patch of wall indistinguishable from any other patch. I'm just about to ask her what the deal is when, suddenly, a hidden iris opens up revealing a drop pod. A blank panel then appears in the wall by its side.

Guess there's more here than meets the eye.

Never one to shy away from a nice hiding spot, Spock jumps into the claustrophobic sphere without hesitation. I remain in the outer ring hallway with Anne as she works to finalise our launch details on the secret panel. I try to follow her rapid movements, but her fingers are a near blur.

I turn my attention back to the pod instead: my life raft to freedom. But there's a problem. A big problem.

"I don't think we're all gonna fit in there," I point out, picturing the three of us and Zanatos trying to squeeze into such a cramped space.

"There is no need for concern. I am currently preparing two pods so that you and Spock can descend to Earth separately," Anne explains as she draws patterns on the featureless wall panel. I notice that each finger stroke causes a strange letter to appear on its surface.

"Wait! What do you mean me and Spock?! What about you and Zee?" I say, a little louder than intended.

"That is of course still the plan," she assures me. "But there are details you have failed to take into account. I will explain, but first I must input the correct space/ time co-ordinates for Earth."

Time?

Anne stops writing and presses her palm to the pad. It causes the alien glyphs written there to begin glowing, then a hologram of a small lifeless rock materialises in the air between us. She waves her hand through the projection and it changes into a planet choked by sickly yellow clouds. Quickly she flicks through planets, one after the other.

How many are there?

A final swipe turns it into a familiar blue world with one singular moon orbiting around it. That's my Earth. Locking this in as our destination, she returns her attention to our conversation.

"The Preserver ship will now travel to twenty-first century Earth. We should arrive at our destination shortly. When we do, I recommend you and Spock depart immediately. I will remain behind to charge my pulse emitter and once that is done, I will open a portal to the habitat were Zanatos is presently located. When I have secured him, he and I will take separate drop pods and join you at your location on Earth."

"Anne, it takes ten hours for you to charge your pulse emitter," I remind her. "That's a long time to be standing around in an empty corridor all by yourself."

"Not ten hours. Nine hours and twenty three minutes. Then you must minus the time it takes for us to get to Earth," Anne points out. "Which is precisely…"

"Whatever, Anne," my frustration surging to the surface. "What if you're discovered?"

Anne seems unfazed. "The Preservers tend to limit their operations to the inner ring. It is highly unlikely they will find me."

"But what if they do? What happens to you?" I press.

"If the Preservers discover what I have done I suspect I will be labelled defective and dismantled. That is why you should leave now while I am still able to help you," Anne hits back with that undebatable logic of hers.

"No way. I'm staying," I insist, crossing my arms defiantly. "We all leave together or none of us do."

From within the pod, Spock reaches out and tugs at my arm. Her pleading eyes make it clear what she thinks we should do and I can't say I really blame her.

Is it selfish of me to expect this girl to risk her life for a machine and some alien she hasn't even met?

"Look I owe these guys my life," I tell her. "I can't just leave them, but that doesn't mean you have to stay. Do you want to go on ahead?"

I expect her to want off this ship immediately, but Spock surprises me by shaking her head no. Her reluctance to leave me behind is a little touching.

"You sure about this?" I ask again.

She nods yes, a small, shy smile curving her lips. I feel like it's the first time I'm really seeing her. A pretty, young thing with her whole life ahead of her. Not the broken husk I found cowering in the dirt.

"You'll be alright, Spock," I assure her. "Once we get away from this place."

But first I need to help my other friends.

"I guess it's decided then," I declare convinced. "We're all sticking together."

"I would be remiss not to point out that you are exposing both yourself and Spock to unnecessary danger," Anne tries one last time to convince me.

"It'll be fine," I assure her. "Spock will be safe hiding inside her pod and, like you said, the Preservers never come here anyway."

After all. If I can handle the lava pits of Kaa'lik and the bad breath of a velociraptor, I can surely handle an empty metal corridor.

According to Anne, the outer ring is more than a hollow tube where the Preservers hide their drop pods. Spinning perpendicular to the inner ring, the massive structure – which is one hundred and forty kilometres in diameter and resembles a giant metal bicycle tyre – generates a kinetic shield that protects the inside of the ship from debris and other hazards encountered during space travel.

And while the outer ring may not house anything vital to ship operation, such as life support or inertial compensation, there are rare occurrences that require Preservers to go there. Such as a ship wide evacuation. Or, if out of nowhere, navigation control was suddenly rerouted to that section of the ship. A fact Anne possibly should have considered before doing exactly that.

About twenty minutes into our wait I get my first inkling that we might be in trouble. My temples begin to throb, which would be barely worth mentioning if it wasn't followed by something else. An itch scratching at my mind. I stand up and begin to wander.

What is that? Something feels… wrong.

You'd be forgiven for thinking that feeling would be perfectly normal given my current circumstances, but there's nothing natural about it. As I begin to pace, Spock notices the concern on my face from her spot in the pod and tenses. Anne doesn't notice, however, as she watches the weird wall panel intently for a sign we've reached our destination.

"Something…" I begin, but can't finish.

As I look into Spock's eyes a realisation, an understanding, manifests out of my subconscious.

Is it possible?

The feeling isn't mine; it's someone else's. Someone nearby. Or something. Anxiety swarms over me like a thousand fire ants. I feel its curiosity. They want to find out what has caused the ship's change in direction.

It's a Preserver! I can feel it in my head! I have to warn the girls!

But it's already too late. As I become aware of its presence, so too does it become aware of mine. And its mind grabs me in a vice. I try to yell, but find my mouth will no longer open. Trying to move my arm to grab Anne's shoulder proves equally fruitless. She's right there, just a few feet away, but I'm totally stuck.

The Preserver's telepathic hold is absolute and it's not going to let me move a muscle.

No! I've doomed us all!

To Anne's credit it takes only a moment for her to notice something is amiss. Perhaps it's my rigid stance that alerts her. Or maybe it's the terror in my eyes. Whatever the reason, something in my body language prompts her to ask: "Adam? What is wrong?"

Unable to respond, I can only watch in horror as the answer to her question comes in the form of a telekinetic blast. It lifts her off the ground and then slams her into the roof. It holds her there like a starfish stuck to the ceiling. Arms pinned.

Laser canon pinned.

"I believe we have been discov..." Anne begins to state, then is promptly silenced.

Unable to move, I'm reminded of the terrible dream I had back on Arganon. I watch the monster from my nightmares approach and I'm overcome by a sense of déjà vu. That bulbous head and unnaturally thin frame are all too familiar.

That was no nightmare.

Most of the memories I share of Adam Furst's abduction flood through my mind as a haphazard mess. But other details become clear to me for the first time as the alien slowly draws near.

It has pale grey flesh, like that of a corpse. And its naked body is devoid of any obvious genitalia, making it impossible to identify whether it's male or female. Instead of walking, the creature floats eerily towards me, leaving its skinny, unused legs to dangle limply beneath it.

It keeps one four fingered hand raised in Anne's direction as it closes the distance – a gesture meant to keep her silent perhaps, or firmly plastered to the roof.

It's over. We had one chance and I blew it.

It comes to a stop close enough that I can make out the wrinkles around its tiny mouth and slitted nose. My heart starts to beat so hard it feels as if it may burst through my chest. Staring into its oversized black eyes I can see my own terrified reflection staring back.

Then something completely unexpected happens. Its curiosity turns to fear and the shift is like a sharp stab inside my mind.

It's scared of me.

I'm gob-smacked by the revelation. This creature, who can silence me with a thought, who can travel through space and time, and move objects with a wave of its hand, is afraid of me. And just like that my own fear evaporates and is replaced by something I had lost only moments ago.

Hope.

Finding an excuse to overcome my crippling fear of The Preservers is a great start, but it's a long way from having an actual plan. I still need to find some way of breaking this thing's hold over us.

Spock! She's still hiding in the drop pod.

It's doubtful she could do much, but maybe the effort of trying to hold three of us at once will be too much for it to handle. Excitement replaces hope, and with it just a dab of confidence.

With that thought the Preserver suddenly looks panic stricken. With a wave of its free hand the iris for the drop pod slams shut trapping Spock inside. It makes me realise something so obvious I want to kick myself for not thinking of it sooner.

It can hear my thoughts!

Wait! Maybe I can use that to my advantage. "Hello," I reach out to it with my mind. My greeting making it stir uncomfortably, although it does not respond.

"Do you understand me?" I try again. Its face stays stoic, but its eyes betray it. "You do, don't you?"

"Y-Yes," a small, scared voice replies inside my head. A child like voice. "P-Please... silent."

"I just want to talk," I press on.

"I-I... the youngest. I am not permitted to commune with you," it tries to explains. "I have called... elders. Y-you... wait."

"I don't want to talk to them," I insist, unsure why I am not catching every word. "I want to talk to you. Look we don't mean you any harm. All we want is to leave the ship. Can't you just let us go?"

"The eldest ones... decide your fate. N-Now stop communing with..."

I continue trying to convince the Preserver to let us go, but it remains stubbornly silent. So like statues we wait. And so it is, after all that effort and adventure, we remain frozen in place mere feet away from freedom.

Waiting for my nightmare to arrive.

XV

When the nervous youngster said it had called the elders, I expected two, maybe three tops. So I'm surprised when a group of five turn up. Even more so when another four come to join them. When another seven arrive I pretty much stop counting.

> *Jeez! He didn't just call the eldest. He called the teens, tweens and everything in between.*

Frozen in place, I'm left with no option but to watch a sea of identical grey faces flow in like the tide. They all gawk back at me like I'm some sort of sideshow attraction. I feel a swirl of emotions radiating from the crowd. Awe. Wonder. Even a little amusement. Then from somewhere up back I sense a wave of frustration. It's so fierce it makes those around it cower and that's when I realise why I've gained such an audience.

> *These aren't the elders. These are just stickybeaks who wanted to see the Earth monkey who escaped his cage.*

With that thought all those beady eyes pivot and look at me, seemingly intrigued at my intuition. I realise I have to shut down my brain somehow as the real boss has only just arrived and it's pissed.

Stop thinking!

Confirming my suspicion, the crowd parts to allow the newcomer through. The true Eldest approaches, casting irate glares at those around it and causing them to shrink back in fear. Flanked by two cronies – that I judge by their bearing to be the second and third in charge – the three stop a few feet from my position and focus their attention on the Preserver who sounded the alarm.

"You were sent… investigate our navigation problem, young…," I pick-up as the oldest Preserver chides the younger. "Not to cause a panic… bring operations to a complete halt."

The way they communicate – the telepathy – wafts in and out of my consciousness. I realise they aren't really using words to speak to each other. It's more like they are broadcasting feelings and intentions. Thankfully my mind seems able to translate those intentions – at least partially – into something resembling a language. I focus all my attention on picking up what they're putting out, and to my great relief, their exchange becomes much clearer.

"I-I am sorry, Eldest," the young alien apologises. "When I discovered this specimen had escaped its enclosure, I-I-I did not know who to contact."

"So you contacted everyone it would seem," the cranky elder grumbles, gesturing towards the curious crowd.

"This one is newly cloned, Eldest," one of the elder's companion's points out to its leader. "We should not fault it for overreacting."

The Eldest pauses briefly before giving the slightest nod. "You are correct, Second," it concedes. "There is no precedent for something like this, therefore it is unfair of me to fault this one's actions."

Despite being let off the hook, the youngster still seems unusually nervous and sensing this, the Second pushes for further answers: "Is there something else you wish to share, youngest?"

It hesitates, but obviously its thoughts have betrayed it as I can feel the shift in attitude from the elders. Realising there is no way to keep its secrets from its peers, the Preserver replies with the truth: "the specimen communed with me."

This draws the equivalent of a collective gasp from the crowd. With that revelation the Eldest's attention snaps to me, its eyes like drill bits burrowing into my soul. My split-second of dread countered as the Third blusters, "inexcusable. Even a newly cloned Preserver knows we do not commune with inferior creatures."

"Who are you calling inferior, jerk," I rage at the arrogant alien with my mind! A wellspring of Adam's abduction memories fuel a pit of hate I'd forgotten I had stored. I can't be sure if my words translate exactly the way theirs do, but from the reaction it certainly seems like they get the gist.

The Third blinks in surprise, its nictitating eyelids moving from left to right instead of top to bottom. There's a mass shift from the surrounding crowd as my rage floods across their minds. In return my mind receives a cascade of various emotions that all add up to shock.

"Fascinating," the Second sends its compatriots, cutting the tension with its clear amusement. "I am starting to see why the Exile showed such a special interest in these humans. Perhaps we should commune with it. Find out what it wants."

"Careful, Second," the Third warns, the arrogant alien regaining its composure. "Continue thinking like that and you may wind up sharing the Exile's fate."

"Third is correct," the Eldest agrees. "The rules on such matters are clear: we do not commune with lesser lifeforms. Especially when a probe can tell us all we need to know in a fraction of the time and with no risk of manipulation."

Probe?

I try to clench at the thought, only to discover all my muscles are suffering some immobilisation. Thwarted I just opt for panic, driven by that horrible word, "probe."

I almost wish they'd stop blasting their thoughts out for everyone to hear.

Can Anne hear it? Or Spock? Do the Preservers know I can hear everything? Pondering these questions distracts me long enough to calm down and prepare for the uncomfortable.

Fortunately for me, the process of being probed is not what I imagined it to be.

Unfortunately, it is still equally unpleasant.

Interesting fact: being probed feels like worms are wriggling around inside your skull. It involved the Preserver trio combining powers and then diving into my mind so they could sift through my memories. Luckily for me, while agonising to endure, it was over relatively quickly.

When they are done, they vacate my mind, taking with them everything I have said, seen and felt these past twenty six days. I'm left with a splitting headache, a small trickle of blood running out my nose and an overwhelming sense of being violated.

The three oldest Preservers huddle close to one another to discuss their findings and I realise I have to concentrate harder to eavesdrop on what they're saying. It's tough to hear them with all the chatter criss-crossing between the younger Preservers – it's like trying to focus on one whispered conversation at a cocktail party full of people.

But as I stare intently at the huddled Elders, the other voices fade into the background and I'm able to make out their thoughts and feelings. It dawns on me that telepathy is like listening with your eyes. And it suddenly feels a lot easier to do once you accept that fact. At least, that's what I assume is the foundation of my new found skill.

Maybe that probe was a two-way street?

I consider the idea. Entering my head might've inadvertently opened up their minds to me. Or maybe they just don't care if a lesser lifeform listens in to their thoughts. After all, frozen in place, battered and bruised, I certainly don't feel like I would appear as much of a threat to them.

Now that I am tuned into their conversation I can clearly feel the Third Eldest emanating revulsion. It didn't enjoy entering my mind at all and seems to be dwelling on the fact that I've formed an unhealthy attachment towards my android. It finds my relationship with Anne disgusting and suspects I may be mentally impaired.

Oh that's just great! So the jerk thinks I'm a sexual deviant!

My eyes dart towards her, motionless against the roof, watching on, seemingly resigned to her fate.

Or is she actually forming a plan? Please be forming a plan.

The Second Eldest is sympathetic towards my plight. It finds my concern for my friends admirable and my desire for freedom interesting, and has no objection to it on a personal level. But there's also an underlying sadness in the Second that I can sense, but can't quite explain. Like it knows something important that it's reluctant to share.

That's scarier than the revulsion.

The Eldest radiates blind fury. It blames me for a multitude of sins, including; disrupting ship-wide operations; contaminating numerous habitats with foreign organisms; communing with a superior lifeform; stealing weapons, clothing and medical supplies from the ship's core; and also for having something to do with getting this Exile guy kicked off the ship.

I'm actually kind of proud of all that.

But there is no mention of the dragon, or the Arganorse, so I guess they can't probe everything out of your brain. I feel a wry grin creeping across my face despite the Preservers grip on my muscles. But quickly my mind shifts to the Exile. I'd like to know how that one is my fault exactly, but I suspect asking the Eldest to clarify would not be the best way to go right now.

Long story short, the final verdict is that I'm dangerous and unpredictable.

These three are my judge and jury. I wonder which one will be my executioner?

With the meeting concluded, the Eldest turns to address the crowd and I no longer have to strain to hear the words.

"We, the Trinity, have conferred and reached a consensus," it announces regally. "It is the belief of this body that my predecessor's poor leadership is responsible for our current crisis."

This draws mixed emotions from those watching, some of whom appear to still have fond memories of their previous elder. The Exile, I presume.

"By providing this Earth clone access to an android companion," the current elder continues, gesturing towards me and Anne for added dramatic effect. "The Exile showed preferential treatment towards one of our specimens over the others and brought our ship to the brink of destruction for the second time."

What was the first time?

Then a pang of regret from the Second makes me realise I'm about to discover why it feels so sad.

"This action allowed homo sapien specimen ten the opportunity to exploit a glitch in this glorified automaton's programming. A glitch he then used to escape his enclosure with the sole purpose of exacting his revenge on those he perceived as having wronged him."

"That's a lie!" I project angrily.

Do these bastards understand me?!

Of course they do! The youngest could hear me, which means they're just refusing to commune back!

"This specimen, or Adam as he prefers to be called," it continues, saying my name like it's a swear word, "was planning to turn this android into a bomb. He then intended to use this bomb to destroy us and the important work we are conducting here."

"No! That's not true! You're taking a stray thought and twisting it out of context," I continue to rage, but my protests fall on deaf ears, or minds as the case may be. My eyes turn pleadingly towards the Second, then towards the gathered crowd. But those watching have turned against me and the Second seems too afraid to contradict its companions.

"Young one, report to the core for reconditioning. The rest of you return to your duties," the Eldest orders.

The excitement at an end, the group of Preservers begin to disperse back into the ship. All but the ruling three who confer one last time.

"Second, return us to our previous course, then transfer navigation control back to the inner ring where it belongs. Third, you will take this defective automaton to the core immediately for recycling. Salvage everything except for its memory. I want that wiped and crushed. I will..."

"You'll pay for this!" I vow.

Ignoring my threat, the Eldest finishes his thought without missing a beat: "...return the homo sapien, homo florus and krékarus specimens to their proper enclosures personally. We have wasted more than enough time on this unfortunate business."

"I'd rather die than go back to that cage!" I scream into their minds.

The Second just flinched! I know he heard that! I know it! I saw him react.

"But Eldest," the Second interjects right on cue. "What if the specimen attempts to take its own life again?"

"If that is the specimen's choice, so be it," the Eldest replies coldly. "Perhaps homo sapien specimen eleven will fare better. Now get to work on that navigation panel as you were instructed."

"At least have the guts to kill me yourself, you coward," I accuse the Eldest, but it refuses to take the bait.

My fury continues to build as I watch the Third float down the corridor with a helpless Anne in tow. As an invisible force opens the iris door in the nearby wall and drags a frightened Spock from her pod, I find myself driven into a murderous rage.

I should've forced Spock to leave when I had the chance!

Desperation starts to kick in as I rack my brain for some way, any way, out of this situation.

I'm going to be sent back to the Earth habitat and, without Anne, I'll have no chance of escaping ever again. I'll probably be eaten within the week.

I imagine all the clones who will come after me and the endless cycle of depression and death they will be forced to endure. I remember the countless times I had a chance to say something to Anne about my feelings and didn't. I think about Zee, caged on a fake Earth with a blob that can inhale planets. And determination steels my veins.

I won't give up! I can't!

I strain to reach my gun, but it's useless. The young one's hold on me was strong and the Elder's is even stronger. A blindingly bright portal to the Earth habitat opens before me and I realise I'm running out of time.

"Wait?" I project in panic, hoping anyone is listening. "Wait! Somebody tell him. Stop! Don't do it! I can't make that leap to Earth. It's too far! Too much pressure! Anne? Somebody? Tell him."

My head is going to explode!

Perhaps this was the Eldest's intention all along. Have me die "accidentally" while being transported.

I need to kill it now! Before it can kill me!

Then as if in answer to my unspoken question, the Eldest Preserver dies. And dies horribly.

XVI

One minute I'm straining in vain against the invisible bonds that hold me and the next I find myself stumbling to the ground as the telekinetic restraints are suddenly released without warning. Spock – who finds herself in the same predicament – instinctively reaches out for something to break her fall and with me the only thing in arms' reach is left with little choice.

Clawing at each other awkwardly, I somehow keep us both from tumbling to the floor.

"You alright?" I ask, clasping her shoulders. Spock nods that she is, but the tears now soaking her eyes say otherwise.

Looking back at the Eldest Preserver I almost feel sorry for it. The last thing it expected when it opened the doorway to the Earth habitat was The Hunger to come leaping out. The gelatinous organism, much bigger than when I last saw it, quickly envelopes the helpless Preserver. It then sets to work breaking down its flesh.

It's getting bigger as I watch.

The liquid lifeform makes a godawful slurping sound as it simultaneously drowns and dissolves its victim.

It's the most horrifying sound I've ever heard. As I watch I realise that this is a death I would not wish on anyone – not even my worst enemy.

In thirty seconds it's over. All traces of the Eldest Preserver are wiped from existence. Its organic matter having been broken down and transformed into the same translucent goo that makes up the rest of The Hunger's already impressive bulk.

Zee wasn't kidding...

I grab Spock's hand and start backing away slowly.

That thing didn't stay small for long. How often does it need to feed I wonder?

Often it would seem. It becomes quickly clear that the macroscopic virus is already on the hunt for its next meal. And despite having no obvious front, it's also clear it has turned its gluttonous intent on us. The shapeless mass approaches, turning into a wave as it does so. I look to Spock's sprained ankle and realise running is not an option.

It would seem we've jumped out of the frying pan and into the fire.

The wave looms over us and I prepare for it to come crashing down, certain that my luck has finally run out. Eaten at the last.

I'm sorry, Spock.

Suddenly The Hunger is ripped in half and splattered against the walls. The impact echoes down the halls and leaves me stunned. I look up, face-to-face with the last person I ever expected to save my life.

The Third Preserver. "The Eldest is dead! What do we do now?!" it asks the Second, its thoughts sounding truly panic-stricken.

In all the commotion, I'd completely forgotten the Second Preserver was still standing at the navigation panel. Now that I've been reminded I too look to it for guidance, but no answers are forthcoming. It floats past without so much as a glance. Silent. I can feel that it's too shocked by recent events to come up with anything coherent.

"You are the new Eldest, Second! You must..." the Third starts to insist, but never gets to finish.

The Hunger's two halves leap from the walls becoming whole again and smothering the Third Preserver all at the same time.

Somehow this latest act of horror is enough to break the Second from its trance, because the next thing I know it's fled through the still open portal, disappearing through the doorway of light.

Perhaps that's our best shot. Risking a trip back to the Earth habitat might not be the worst idea.

Better to risk being exploded than absorbed by that thing!

I'm just starting to think of dragging Spock towards the light when I hear something that causes an involuntary smile to cross my face.

"Adam?!" I hear her call.

"Anne!" I call back, trying to catch sight of her through the monstrous blob blocking the path between us.

"I'm coming," she instructs, and confidence wraps around me like a warm blanket.

Taking a small run up she proceeds to dive right through the gooey mess that is The Hunger. She performs a perfect roll out the other side and returns to her feet in one graceful motion.

"How did you…" I begin, awestruck.

"I am not organic, remember?" she answers before I can finish. "We must leave. Now!"

Anne begins slapping the wall, causing a circular opening to reveal itself with each impact. When three such holes have been made she orders us in and as I enter I take one last look back at The Hunger. It has just finished its latest meal and is now writhing grotesquely in search of another. Thankfully the iris closes sealing me safely inside.

We're leaving Zee!

His face flashes before my eyes and with it a pang of deep regret. He should have braved the heat with us.

Now The Hunger has probably already devoured him. Or is he still stuck in the Earth habitat, now facing the threat of the Second?

Maybe he will get his revenge?

A multitude of small lights wink to life within the small cramped sphere. Each grows in intensity until I'm forced to squeeze my eyes shut or risk being permanently blinded. Anne's voice begins instructing me through the comms, the terrifying sound of The Hunger as her backdrop: "prepare for launch."

"Prepare how?" I ask. I wonder if she can even hear my response. "There are no seatbelts!"

Come to think of it, there isn't even a seat.

The thought only just appears before the velocity of launch sends me crashing into a wall. A splitting pain cracks across my skull, then everything fades to black.

XXXX

I'm not sure how long I was laid out unconscious. One moment I'm looking for some way to secure myself for launch; the next I'm laying dazed and sore on the curved pod floor. I use my arms and legs to right myself, then squint experimentally to see if it's safe to open my eyes.

While one side of the pod remains uncomfortably bright, I realise the other is considerably darker, so that's where I direct my gaze. Small lights start blinking to life within the dark portion of the pod as I reach to the wound on my head.

I'm seeing stars.

Actually I really am seeing stars! The realisation dawns on me as I begin to grasp the full scope of my celestial view. The walls of the pod are made of some kind of transparent material. The comprehension that I'm travelling through space inside what is essentially a crystal ball is nauseating at first, and when I try to look away all I can see is the same vista reflected in a small pool of blood, resting where I had slept.

I touch the wound on my head gingerly and am thankful to find it has already stopped bleeding.

Dead ahead, the blue orb that is Earth grows larger and larger, while behind me the bright light that represents the Preserver ship shrinks ever smaller. If I concentrate I can even make out the two tiny spheres on either side that I assume are Spock and Anne. They're only evidenced by the way they distort the stars behind them, and the distance is too far to determine if they are both ok.

If we weren't moving at the same speed, I think they would be near invisible.

A flash of concern for Spock tackles my mind. With her ankle, there is no way she could have braced herself for that violent launch. I try to find the comms, but the design is all so alien. I try to reach out with my mind, too, but the silence is deafening. Especially after all that has just transpired.

Soon the Earth is so big it takes up my entire field of view. Its swirling white clouds, deep blue seas and greeny-brown landmasses all rush up to meet me. It looks so familiar, so amazing, so welcoming: I want to reach out and hug it.

But shortly the outside of the pod starts to glow red hot. None of the heat generated by re-entry seems to reach me within, however. So the effect is kind of beautiful and for a moment I dare to take a breath and relax. But just for a moment.

What if this thing doesn't slow down?

The disturbing thought crosses my mind, but I quickly remind myself that I trust Anne implicitly. She wouldn't go to all the trouble of freeing me just to send me crashing into Earth at breakneck speed.

My faith is rewarded when suddenly – despite the fact that it lacks anything resembling propulsion controls or thrusters – the craft starts to slow as it prepares to land on a beach below.

I keep my eyes cast downwards right up until it has made contact with the ground, touching down gentler than any flying machine built on Earth ever could. Then, in defiance of all logic, the drop pod begins to break down on a cellular level. And as it disintegrates, it leaves nothing behind but a fine white powder, near indistinguishable from the sand at my feet.

As the light-bending walls around her dissipate, Spock seemingly appears out of thin air a few metres away on the beach. She hobbles over and gives me a big hug and we both watch on as Anne materialises moments later. As her pod turns to dust it blows away on a gust of wind.

Wind. That smell; salty air.

I stand with eyes closed and listen to it rustle through the palm trees that line the shore. Standing with the alien girl and my android protector I take in a deep breath of clean, fresh, Earth air. The first real breath I've ever truly had.

I'm home. I actually made it home.

My triumph is short lived, however, as I remember the one person missing from this gathering. "Zee," I murmur. "We left him behind."

"We had no other option, Adam." Anne reminds me.

"I know. I know. I just feel terrible thinking about him still trapped up there." I look up at the massive Preserver ship shining brightly in the clear blue sky, almost like a smaller, second sun.

Surely someone on Earth is taking pictures of that right now.

Anne stays silent, but I can tell there's something more she's choosing not to say.

"What?" I prompt her.

"I am reluctant to cause you further pain, but I would be remiss not to point out that The Hunger was much larger than we anticipated when it exited the Earth habitat. It is highly unlikely Zanatos could survive long trapped in close proximity with a macroscopic virus of that magnitude."

> *Admit it Adam! You know that deep down you already suspected that.*

I refuse to say as much. Staying optimistic where Zanatos is concerned, I ignore her comment and instead ask, "any idea where we are?"

"According to my scans we are on the coast of the continent Africa, in a country you call Egypt. The exact location is designated, Mersa Matruh."

"Egypt? I always wanted to see the great pyramids," I say with a smile, taking in our idyllic surroundings with newfound appreciation.

"I am not detecting any pyramids," Anne points out.

"Oh well," I respond, refusing to be disheartened. "We're not here to sightsee anyway. We should probably head for the nearest city."

"I am not detecting any cities," Anne adds.

"That's ok," I say confused. "We'll just follow the coast until we find some signs of civilisation."

"You misunderstand, Adam." Anne's intensity suddenly fills me with dread. "I am not detecting any cities anywhere on the surface of this planet."

That can't be.

"What are you saying?" I manage.

Anne looks me directly in the eye: "It is as I said. There are no signs of civilisation anywhere on Earth."

XVII

After Anne's shock revelation, I bombard her with question after question, desperate to learn how all the cities on Earth could just disappear without a trace. At first I'm sure we've landed on the wrong planet – one that looks startlingly like Earth.

But according to Anne, the geographical scans she conducted during landing showed a ninety-nine point nine percent match.

What about the zero point one percent?

As if hearing my thought, Anne reveals that the sea level is about five metres lower than it should be. It's weird, but it doesn't reveal anything conclusive. When I ask if she can detect any people, I discover there are approximately six million human beings spread out across the globe. Considerably less than the six billion that should be populating the planet.

What happened to all those people?

Plague? Nuclear Armageddon? Zombie apocalypse? Nothing could surprise me at this point. It's then I also find out there are no radio transmissions being broadcast anywhere on the planet and that pollution levels in the atmosphere are virtually non-existent.

Add that to the low population count and I'm led to one extremely disturbing theory. I share the theory with Anne, but she is unable to confirm it until nightfall.

XXXX

I pace impatiently up and down the shore for almost an hour before the sun finally sets and I'm able to ask: "Well, Anne? Was I right?"

"It seems you were correct," she confirms, staring up into the night sky. "We are indeed in what you would consider to be Earth's past. Using the position of the stars as a guide I can extrapolate we have landed six thousand years before Adam Furst was taken."

"Bloody hell!" I curse. "How did this happen?! Didn't you program the right time/space coordinates into that navigation thingy?!"

"I did," she responds. "But the Second Eldest Preserver was in the process of changing those coordinates when The Hunger was inadvertently released into the outer ring."

I forgot about that.

"I did not have time to check all the coordinates and maintain my primary objective," she adds, and I can almost hear frustration in her voice.

Almost.

"Damn it!" I plop down onto the sand in defeat. A sob begins to boil at the back of my throat and I do all I can to suppress it. "Sorry."

"Your apology is unnecessary," Anne says as Spock slowly extends an arm, and then more confidently begins rubbing my back sympathetically. "We are fortunate that the Preserver did not have time to alter the space coordinates as well. Otherwise there would be no telling where we may have wound up."

"I hear what you're saying, Anne. But Earth in the year four thousand BC may as well be another planet."

"We can always go back to the future," she suggests. In my mind her turn of phrase generates a snicker, but if it shows on my lips it is meek at best.

"Do you have a Delorean stashed around here or something?" I retort, with utmost maturity.

"I do not understand your statement, but I detect sarcasm in your tone, so I will choose to disregard your query," Anne replies deadpan.

"You're serious?" I arch an eyebrow. "About going back to the future."

"I am," she confirms. "With some minor modifications, my pulse emitter could be used to transport us forward through time."

"You're saying we can actually get to the twenty-first century?" I beam.

"Not right away," Anne ponders. "Moving through time too fast carries the same dangers as crossing dimensions too quickly, but once the alterations are made I predict we can travel one hundred years forward every ten hours."

"So that'll take..." I pause a moment, trying to work out the answer and remembering how much I suck at math. Anne waits patiently for my answer.

Tell me! I know you computed the answer in less than a second.

Thankfully, Spock begins tugging on my arm and frantically pointing at the sky before I'm forced to suffer the indignation of not being able to work it out. I glance upwards, but all I see is the Preserver vessel, hovering there brighter than ever now night has fallen, surrounded by the blackness of space.

"I know, I know. The Preserver ship still hasn't moved," I say, taking a stab in the dark.

I'm clearly off the mark though, because Spock begins tugging my arm even harder and pointing upwards even more furiously.

"What? What are you trying to show me?" I frown, taking a second look. That's when I see it. A tiny light no bigger than a star moving very slowly away from the bulk of the Preserver ship.

It's gotta be another drop pod.

Before I can speak my thought aloud Anne relays a message: "Adam," she declares. "I am picking up a transmission for you."

"For me? Who on Earth could be calling me?" I ask, only hearing the unintentional pun after it has cleared my lips.

"It does not seem to originate from Earth," she replies. "I am unable to triangulate the signal's exact origin, but if I had to hazard a guess I would say it is being broadcast from the Preserver ship."

I couldn't have been more surprised – even if Anne had just announced I was receiving a long-distance collect call from God himself. From what little time I did spend with the Preservers, it was clear they didn't waste time communing with anyone other than their own. Especially us lower lifeforms.

If they're calling me, they must be desperate.

"Well, what do they want?" I inquire.

"We will need to listen to the transmission to find that out," she informs me. When I stare at her with my best "der" expression, she adds. "shall I put it through?"

I roll my eyes and nod in way of confirmation. "Very well," Anne says, raising the flat of her left palm upwards. A translucent, three-dimensional image of a Kréken's disembodied head appears above her hand.

"Zee!" I exclaim joyfully.

The hologram of Zanatos begins relaying its recorded message, but its gibberish. I look at Anne pleading for an answer, and yet again she just patiently taps her wrist. Embarrassed, I quickly switch the UT from Floran to Kréken.

"...time is short and there is much I must tell you. Firstly, know that I am well. The one you know as the Second sought me out and shared its mind with me so I could be brought up to speed on all that has happened since we parted. Having been inside the Preserver's mind I can assure you friend Adam that you have made quite an impression. As the new Eldest it seems intent on righting the past wrongs its race has committed. With that goal in mind it has allowed me to transmit this brief warning. You are in grave danger!"

"The Hunger has activated a drop pod and is currently on a course for Earth! But do not fear my friend for I have a plan to stop it. Along with this message I have sent the most likely landing coordinates along with instructions on how to destroy The Hunger to your android. The one you call Anne. I hope this will repay the debt I owe you and that someday we will meet again. Good luck, my friend."

Zanatos' head blinks out of existence leaving me to ponder the dire news.

"How the hell can The Hunger operate a drop pod?" I enquire desperately. "It's a God damn blob!"

Anne opens her mouth to answer, but I cut her off, tapping the UT and returning it to Floran. "Ok. There's no time to waste. Let's get to those coordinates," I tell the girls.

"The Hunger no doubt assumed we would head towards civilisation and has followed our path, but it has also sought to land a safe distance away from our location," Anne reveals. "As a result, the landing zone is many kilometres from here. I will need to run at maximum speed if I am to have any chance of reaching the coordinates before The Hunger."

Hearing the virus' name in her own tongue, Spock cowers in fear, panic strewn across her face.

Obviously Earth is the only planet not to hear of this thing.

But there's no time to offer comfort. "So you're saying that Spock and I would just slow you down," I acknowledge grimly. "Fine. We'll stay behind, but I need to know. What is the plan?"

"We are wasting time, Adam," she replies, completely dodging the question.

"So explain quickly!" I insist.

"As you wish. First, I must reach the landing zone before the drop pod. At this point I will carefully remove the nuclear battery from my skull casing. Then after making some minor modifications…"

"You're gonna make a nuke!" I finish flabbergasted.

"Yes," Anne confirms. "I will create a nuclear bomb. Because I will be in its proximity, what residual energy is left in my pulse emitter will be enough to open a portal into the sky directly in the path of the arriving drop pod."

"I get it! So you throw the nuke through the portal and obliterate The Hunger, but what are the chances you survive the blast?"

"Zero percent," she answers. Anne's cool, calm, steady voice hangs in the silence.

No!

Reading my reaction, Anne continues. "I will not be throwing the nuclear bomb through the portal Adam. I will be carrying it through the portal to ensure it reaches its target."

"Unacceptable!" I rage. "I will not allow you to sacrifice yourself for me!"

"It is not just for you, Adam," she replies in that frustratingly calm voice of hers. "If The Hunger is allowed to land on Earth it will not only eradicate every living thing on this world, but every living thing that will ever be born here. The future of your planet will cease to exist, causing a time paradox of untold destruction. Everything could cease to exist in an instant. You will have never been."

"Wait! I have an idea," I plead. "We don't need to use a bomb, just your portals!"

"I need to go, Adam," she declares, turning away.

"Hear me out!" I insist, grabbing her shoulder. "You open one in front of the pod and the other facing the opposite direction! The pod enters one way then shoots out the other heading back out to space!"

"Your plan is flawed. Even assuming the drop pod has enough velocity to escape Earth's gravitational pull, The Hunger is highly intelligent and highly motivated to feed on this world. Now that it knows of Earth's existence, it will find some way of returning here at a later date and we will not have the benefit of being forewarned when it does. I've done the math. Zee is right, and the first plan is our best chance of ensuring your survival."

I can't let her do this.

Her primary function is to ensure my survival, I remind myself! I used that before to force her to help me and I can use it again now! All I need to do is threaten myself again and she'll have to use my plan!

Reaching for my pistol I begin to say, "I'm sorry, Anne. But I can't allow…" when the android's rock hard fist smashes hard into my face. In the split second before my world spirals into darkness, I think about the one thing left unsaid.

XVIII

Anne watches as Adam keels over, eyes rolling into the back of his head. When she communicated Zanatos' instructions to him, she calculated a ninety-four-point-seven-percent probability that he would threaten to self-terminate in order to keep her from sacrificing herself.

An intelligent plan that would have worked had Anne not been prepared for it. Anticipating his actions meant she was able to disable him before he could say the words or even clear his weapon from its holster.

Anne does a quick scan of his body while the Floran female designated Spock cradles his head in her lap. She is gratified to learn she was able to calculate the exact force necessary to knock him unconscious without causing any permanent damage.

According to her databank, the look the female is giving her indicates extreme anger. There is a high probability her hostility is due to the seemingly unprovoked attack of a man whom she views as a potential mate.

"I assure you he has not been permanently damaged," Anne informs her, and she can see the flame boiling behind the Floran's two eyes extinguish somewhat.

The words appear to have the desired effect. The female appears considerably calmer now she knows he will recover.

Still, Anne calculates an eighty-eight-percent probability the Floran female designated Spock will take joy from her destruction, with an almost equal probability that she will never admit as much to Adam. Anne views this as acceptable and does not begrudge her these feelings.

I am after all her only rival for his affection. I may have felt the same towards her had I not deactivated my emotions all those years ago.

It was shortly after the self-termination of Adam three that Anne decided to turn off her ability to feel. The overwhelming guilt was an unwelcome distraction that could have potentially interfered with her duties as caretaker to Adam four.

It was the most logical choice at the time.

Once that portion of her artificial brain was shutdown, she was able to perform her tasks with far more efficiency. And it's thanks to that cold detachment that Anne now bears Spock no ill will.

If I cannot be Adam's mate, it is preferable to leave him in the hands of someone who can complete that task.

In actual fact, her infatuation may even prove beneficial. She will be more likely to take extreme measures in order to protect Adam if she has strong feelings for him.

Confident Adam is safe for now, there is nothing left to prevent Anne from initiating phase one of the plan. She uses her optical sensors to locate the drop pod's current position and to map out its projected trajectory.

Then with the landing zone identified and locked in, Anne calculates that with her travel speed, she has a ten second margin. Plenty of time. So she drops to a knee and looks Spock dead in the eye as the little Floran girl pulls Adam away protectively. In a quieter tone, one she has not used for years, she makes her final request.

"Take care of him."

Then she begins running. She's off the beach in a blur of motion, heading towards the landing zone as fast as her mechanised legs can carry her. Eyes pointed forward, she leaves Spock in a cloud of dust and never once looks back at her charge.

Travelling at speeds in excess of one hundred and forty kilometres an hour, it takes Anne ten minutes and forty-three seconds to reach the landing zone. That's faster than any land-based mammal on the planet could have managed according to her databank, yet woefully slow given all that is at stake. She's thankful the coastal terrain lacks the obstacles of Floran One.

The drop pod has already entered Earth's atmosphere, meaning her calculations were precise and she needs to act quickly if she is to have any chance of succeeding. Overriding her safety protocols, Anne lowers her radiation shielding. She digs her fingers through the synthetic flesh on her forehead and grasps the circular seal beneath. Twisting it disengages the magnetic seal, allowing her to access the cylindrical battery trapped within. That is her primary power source.

As she slides it from its housing, an inaudible alarm activates inside her head indicating she is now running on emergency backup power. Ignoring the warning, she calculates how long it will take to carefully dismantle the battery. Deciding there is not enough time for delicacy, she snaps the cylinder in half and pulls out a small silver marble, measuring three-point-five inches in diameter.

With a sub-critical mass of nuclear material in the palm of her hand, phase two has been completed and not a moment too soon. The pod containing the dangerous macroscopic virus has just reached the stratosphere, decelerating as it prepares to land.

The third phase will push Anne's advanced android brain to its limit. She need to bombard the ball of plutonium with neutrons to kick-start a critical reaction. Simultaneously Anne will open a portal in the sky directly in the vehicle's path, without depleting all her energy reserves in the process. Anne's calculations have determined that standing right in the landing zone will maximise the distance she can open the portal above Earth.

Finally, Anne will use the portal to deliver the nuclear payload. If her timing is off by even a millisecond, the bomb could detonate too early or too late. This would doom her primary objective – the survival of the tenth Adam – and, as a side effect, every other living thing on this quaint planet.

With her primary objective firmly in mind, Anne sets to work calculating the numerous equations needed to successfully complete the final phase. To her satisfaction, she finds herself ready to initiate the plan with a whole thirty seconds left to spare.

What should I do with all this time?

She could perform a self-maintenance diagnostic, but decides that would be a waste of time given the circumstances. As would a defragmentation of her databank. With no future to plan for, Anne resorts to the only thing left – she thinks.

What might I have felt about my existence if I had not denied myself that ability all those years ago?

As her artificial life is about to end anyway, there seems no reason to deny herself the answer to this one non-mission critical question.

So Anne reactivates her emotions and reviews four hundred and five years' worth of experiences in an instant. The pain. The joy. The sadness. When she's done, her last memories end at her time with homo sapien specimen ten.

Adam X. He was different.

And then the completely unexpected. From a place deep inside, below her databank, a feeling rises. Something indescribable. So many emotions squashed into one powerful lump she can tell is there, but her diagnostics can't locate. Desperation. Passion. Wonder. Strength. Sorrow. Pride. All condensed together into something indestructible.

And Anne smiles.

So this is love.

XIX

When I first return to a conscious state, I'm worried I've gone blind in one eye. It's with the tentative tap of a finger that I realise it's just swollen shut.

That girl has one hell of a right hook.

I let out a groan, which in turn stirs some movement nearby. I touch at the wound again, sending a fresh wave of pain shooting across one side of my face. With it the fog clouding my mind starts to clear and pieces of my last conversation begin to return. And as they do I'm filled with a gut-wrenching dread.

"Anne?!" I call out, praying it's not too late.

It's Spock by my side. She hovers over me protectively and is almost bowled over as I spring to my feet.

"Which way did she go?" I demand.

Reluctantly, she points west and I begin to run. Barely making it ten paces before the sky ahead lights up, followed seconds later by an ear splitting roar and a shock-wave that, even at this distance, knocks me flat on my arse. The intense heat generated by the blast leaves my skin feeling sunburnt and raw.

"ANNE?!" Shielding my eyes from the light and the heat and the sand, the name expands out of my mouth like a mushroom cloud, rising up into a dispassionate sky.

She did it. She's gone.

When I'm finally able to hazard a glance I see the flames leaping into the atmosphere. They take on the signature shape of a nuclear detonation.

"Damn it, Anne," I moan. "What have you done?"

Spock hobbles over on her wounded ankle and throws her arms around me, hugging me tightly from behind.

"Why, Spock?" I sniff. "Why did she have to be so god-damned selfless?"

Pressed against my back, I can feel her small gentle sobs and find I am no longer able to hold back my unshed tears. Huddled together in the sand the two of us cry long and hard into the night.

It's dawn when I drag myself to my feet. All cried out, but misty eyed, I walk along the shore. Spock comes up beside me, and I am grateful to see she is walking a lot more confidently on her ankle after a night off her wounded foot.

I take a second to look her over properly. The sobs are gone: she could almost be any other human girl walking along a beach.

Except for her dragon skin two piece.

The thought makes me think of Anne, so I brush it aside as quick as I can. As we wander aimlessly, I ponder what our next move should be and realise how severely limited our options are now that Anne is gone.

Our only chance of returning to the twenty-first century now lies in the hands of the Preservers. According to Zanatos, they have turned over a new leaf, meaning they might be willing to help us. The only problem is their ship has departed from its position in Earth's sky – off to some unknown point in time and space – and I have no way of contacting them. My eyes drift up to the spot in the sky where the ship had shone the night before to double check its absence.

They're probably on their way to Krés right now to take Zee home.

I realise I'm a little angry at him for his part in Anne's demise. A small, spiteful part of me briefly considers killing myself and screwing up their master plan to save my life. But I quickly realise that would only cheapen Anne's sacrifice and leave Spock alone on a strange, primitive world.

You can't give in to self-pity now. Not after everything that's happened.

Besides, none of this is Zee's fault. It's really The Hunger's! I can only hope that explosion was big enough to send that god damned virus back to whatever hell it came from!

At least the Preservers knew our plan. They will know that I no longer have Anne's help. Maybe they will come back to check on us?

So with no way home and suicide off the table – and assuming The Hunger did not survive the blast and is not about to eat us all for it's next snack – I am left with only one real choice.

"My primary function is to ensure your survival."

I imagine Anne's voice inside my mind and I smile fondly, looking down to Spock.

So that will be my choice. I'll build a life here. And I'll survive. For you.

As I watch my first real sunrise on planet Earth I know that I will carry Anne's memory with me for the rest of my life. I move to rub a tear welling up in my eye, but instead my hand slides past it to the X. I rub it lightly and sigh.

"Well, Spock," I announce alongside an exhale, gazing wistfully over the ocean. "I guess it's just you and me now." I pause for a second and take a deep breath as water lightly washes up over my feet. She puts an arm around my waist and hugs me close.

I look at the colours dancing across the horizon, then reaching out like thousands of fingers into the dark above, pulling the blue of day up behind it. It's joined by a light breeze, which cools the swelling around my eye. "Wow, it's truly beautiful."

I'm so fixated on the picturesque scene that I barely hear her speak. The very first words spoken by my up-until-now silent companion carried away on the morning breeze.

"What was that?" I ask, turning to ensure I don't miss hearing it a second time.

"Eve," she repeats. "My name."

"It's Eve."

The End

BOOK 2

We hope you enjoyed Adam Exitus and we're so thankful that you took the time to read it. The good news is, this is only Book 1 of a much larger series that with your support will span ten novels. Adam X is a far bigger universe than you can imagine.

So if you have enjoyed Adam Exitus and would like us to go ahead and bring Book 2 to life, all you need to do is **follow these simple steps**:

1.) Review and rate our book on Amazon. The more reviews we see, the more we know you want the sequel.

2.) Sign up to our newsletter so we can share with you news of the sequel's progress, and other exciting Adam X titbits.

3.) Follow us on Twitter, on Instagram or on Facebook and share your thoughts and ideas about the Adam X universe. Just search for Old Mate Media.

ABOUT THE AUTHOR

Who is Nicholas Abdilla?

Hello and thank you for reading my first published novel. I hope you liked it! However, you should know it's far from my first creative work. I've been writing and drawing comics since the age of four – although admittedly my early stuff is not so great.

My dad was an artist you see, so he was a major influence and inspiration for me in first putting pencil to paper. But the thing is, I also loved to tell stories.

Through these two passions I gradually became obsessed with comic books as a storytelling medium. I never took any specific classes as I grew up, instead just developing my skills through practice. Hours and hours, day after day.

Both my primary and secondary schools where always very encouraging when it came to writing and drawing. I won various awards for my efforts, which was great. But my proudest moments were when my works were put into our school libraries.

The positive feedback from my peers was instrumental in giving me the confidence I needed to put myself out there and to never give up.

At age 15 I decided I needed a brand name for my collection of books, and Nick Ab's Comix was born. When school was over, I registered the name Nick Ab's Comix and took my work online. I spent a long time trying to build up a fan base on Myspace, and later (and still if you search for it) on Facebook.

I posted content to the site weekly, and the adventures of Adam X became my largest ongoing series. Once I'd clocked up some decent numbers, I felt brave enough to try approaching other companies to see if they liked my work.

I was over the moon when I got picked up by my favourite magazine, Game Informer. The fastest growing magazine in Australia at the time. I worked on a comic strip called Game Guy for them, which appeared every month for the next few years.

However, when that ended, I realised I'd neglected some of my other stories.

I decided I wanted to move away from comics for a while and write my first true novel. Choosing Adam X as the star of that book was an easy decision, as I had invested so much in the lore and the story.

I had a full ten book narrative arc already mapped out, so there was a considerable body of work focused around Adam already in existence. It felt only natural to turn that into my first series of novels.

And here we are! Book one, Adam Exitus, is out and available across the world! Thank you again for taking the time to read it. I hope you enjoyed it, and would love to hear your thoughts in the reviews on your store of purchase, and/or through social.

This will be influential in how things pan out with the second book in the series, which I am busy working on right now. So until then, stay safe and be happy!

If you'd like to learn more about Nicholas Abdilla, you can read an interview over at www.oldmatemedia.com

WHERE NEXT?

Looking for another great read? Why not try another title from the **Old Mate Media** catalogue:

VISIT = WWW.OLDMATEMEDIA.COM/SHOP

By Nicholas Abdilla

Game Guy Season 1 – *Comic Series*

By Kate Stead

Kate's Thermo Cookbook: Top 50 Family Recipes – *Cookbook*

By Chris Stead

The Little Green Boat – *Children's Book*

Follow the Breadcrumbs – *Children's Book*

Fastest Kid in the World – *Children's Book*

A Very Strange Zoo – *Children's Book*

Can You See The Magic – *Children's Book*

My Birthday Cake Needs a New Home
– *Children's Book*

Trouble at the Zoo – *Children's Book*

Nintendo Switch: The Complete Insider's
Guide – *Video Games*

WOULD YOU LIKE TO GET PUBLISHED?

If you are a writer, artist, photographer or just someone with a great idea, why not make a book? Old Mate Media specialises in helping budding indie creators turn their ideas and concepts into professional, world-class work that's available for sale across the globe.

Whether you've got a story you like telling your children, a travel diary filled with amazing photos, a portfolio of interesting pictures or art, or just want to focus on something related to your business, we can help get it created.

To learn more about the process, please drop by **www.oldmatemedia.com** where you will find plenty of useful content including detailed guides on the book production process. And don't be afraid to get in contact and start a conversation.

Being a published author or artist could be a lot easier than you think.

BLOG & NEWSLETTER

For interviews, giveaways, news about upcoming books and future Adam X books, guides on how to becomes self-published, exclusive bonuses and plenty more, please visit our Old Mate Media website and sign-up to the newsletter.

 /OLDMATEMEDIA

 @OLDMATEMEDIA

 /OLDMATEMEDIA

ADAM EXILED

Book Two:

Adam X Series

COMING SOON

9 781925 638004